PERSONAL JUSTICE

This book is a work of fiction. Any names, characters, places or incidents contained herein are strictly products of the authors' imaginations and are used in a fictitious scenario. Any resemblance to any actual person or persons, living or dead, or real situations is purely coincidental.

For more information on Chuck Bush, visit
http://www.facebook.com/chuckbushstoryteller
Click "Sign Up" to join our mailing and receive exclusive,
first-look content.

Dedication

I am dedicating this book to two fellas in my life that inspire me. To my dad, Charlie "Doc" Bush, Jr., who died earlier this year. I think he would have been proud. And to my son, Brennen, whose story inspired me to create this fiction.

Also, to C.C. and Kay. Thank you for your tireless work and amazing contribution to this book. Couldn't have done it without you.

CHAPTER 1

Sweat formed on Amelia's forehead as the cold barrel of the pistol pressed against her skin. She had seen his silhouette at the foot of her bed only a few seconds earlier, but her fear prevented her from moving, screaming; and now there was no stopping him.

She looked up at his face, covered in darkness. Did she know him? She couldn't make out the details on the countenance of this man standing over her, pressing a gun to her head. Her first thought was to beg him for her life, but her fear quickly turned to anger, and she glared up at him. She wasn't about to go down without a fight.

Seconds felt like minutes, as her assailant's whitened knuckle wrapped around the trigger and squeezed. Amelia screamed as a shot rang out.

She bolted upright in bed, sweat-drenched, clasping her head between her trembling hands. It felt so real like all the others.

She kept checking to make sure her head was still intact. It was just another dream. A nightmare she just couldn't seem to get used to. She struggled to catch her breath as she fumbled to find the bedside lamp. The light came on; Amelia squinted.

She threw off the covers and rolled her feet onto the floor. She bent over, placed her head between her knees, and attempted to slow her erratic breathing. She had goosebumps on her arms, as her nightgown was cold and wet against her ebony skin.

"This is ridiculous," she whispered to herself. "You've *got* to get over this."

Amelia sat on the side of her bed, arms now crossed in a self-soothing hug. She rocked back and forth. Amelia knew it was only a dream, so why did she feel like screaming? Or, God forbid, crying? For the first time in a long time, Amelia Melchor felt alone and afraid. It scared her to realize these emotions, emotions that made her appear weak and vulnerable, were so close to the surface; close enough to show.

Amelia looked at the clock on her bedside table. It read 2:26. She reached for her phone, and it rang in her hand. It startled her, and she fumbled and almost dropped it.

She put the phone to her ear and answered without looking at the caller ID. "This better not be a booty call; I'm so not in the mood."

She listened as the caller stated their name. "Oh I'm so sorry." Amelia rolled her eyes, "Usually a call at this hour is either bad news or well, you know."

"How bad is it?" She asked and waited for the reply.

"Ok, I'll be there in a bit. I can't sleep anyway. Let the police know I will see them soon."

Amelia ended the call and placed her phone back on the nightstand. She reached for a pillow and hugged it close to her stomach for a few moments, thinking about the dream, and then the phone call.

"No rest for the wicked," she thought to herself. She stuffed her feelings of fear and vulnerability like a pro, stood up, threw the pillow onto the bed and headed for the shower.

CHAPTER 2

Amelia nodded to the police officer standing watch on the street as though she recognized him. She stepped under the crime scene tape that roped off the sidewalk leading to her office. She waved to the window repairman who was waiting near the door. "Thanks for coming over so quickly Mr. Abel. Again."

He waved back and responded with, "No problem, Ms. Melchor. Now my kid has hopes of going to college, thanks to your insurance company."

"Glad I could help." She half-grinned back at him before going into the building.

Glass *crunched* under her Prada shoes in a symphony of disdain as she walked through her open law office door. Amelia glanced down at the million pieces of the window that once held the words, "*Melchor and Associates, L.L.P.*" Some of them flickered like stars in the evening sky reflecting various sources of light as Amelia navigated the damage.

She walked into her office and took in the scene. A policeman with a jacket that had the letters CSU on the back was busy digging at the wall behind her desk. The detective who was standing behind her chair acknowledged her with a chin check, nothing more. Again, this was familiar.

Amelia raised her hand and ran it along the tight bun she wore, smoothing invisible stray hairs. She glanced into the mirror that hung on her office wall and wondered if her appearance completely belied her truth.

"Good morning, Detective Johnson." She greeted him without taking her eyes off of her reflection.

"So the fan club strikes again, I see," responded Detective Trey Johnson.

"They are devoted," she replied dryly as she turned and looked over the crime scene technician's shoulder. He finished taking measurements with his tape, put his right hand under his chin and queried.

"How tall are you, Ms. Melchor?"

"5 foot 5," she responded quizzically. "Don't even think about asking my weight," she added in humorous subterfuge. The crime scene unit was momentarily amused.

"Why is that important?" Amelia asked.

"Your bullet hit in just the right place..." the tech stammered. Amelia shot him a puzzled look.

"What I mean is, apparently the shooter had been here before. He knew exactly where you would've been sitting." He pointed to her chair, and wiggled his finger in the bullet hole that went clean through. "This was meant to be a head shot."

Detective Johnson floated a theory, "Would you say that could be construed as some kind of warning, Keaton?"

The crime scene tech didn't hesitate, "…of the deadliest kind, Detective." Trey looked at Amelia to see if she caught his inference. Apparently not.

Amelia cocked an eyebrow, as she stared at her chair. "Remind me not to work past midnight anymore." Her tone was sarcastic, but her eyes flickered with fear. The tech smiled at her, uncomfortable with her quip.

Detective Johnson let out a breath and shook his head, then motioned for her to step out into the hallway. His brow was furrowed and a look of concern crept over his face. He reached for her arm. "Amelia..."

She backed away from him, held up a hand and shook her head. "We are not going to do this, Trey."

He dropped his hands to his side and cleared his throat. "Ms. Melchor...if you are waiting for a horse's head to turn up in your bed before you finally *get it*, well that's your prerogative. I'm serious as a heart attack when I tell you this is one admirer you do not want! Can't you see how this is escalating?"

Amelia sighed and rolled her eyes. She leaned against the wall, crossed her arms, and stared at him while he spoke. Amelia was very deliberate with her body language, and she let *it* do her talking for the moment.

Trey continued, "Being honest, you know there's no great love lost between the department and your firm, given your past clientele. I understand it takes a certain…*personality type* to do what you do, but this is a new level of stubborn, even for you!"

She turned her head and stared down the hall. She appeared to have tuned him out, so he could just talk to the back of her head.

"Hey, do us both a favor and take a vacation. This is the fifth incident in six weeks, and frankly, that's a record I don't want to own, alright? Your little fan club has graduated from bricks to bullets. Take a hint!"

She turned to face him. "First of all, each of my clients have constitutional rights and are innocent until proven guilty. And here's a newsflash, Detective. I'm in Family Court now, remember?"

He leaned closer to her as he strained to keep his voice down. "Oh yeah, that kinder, gentler practice of law. Adultery, spousal abuse, murder for hire; I see the difference now."

"Right...well instead of worrying about who my clients are or were, why don't we focus on the task at hand and deal with this *inconvenient distraction*, okay?" Trey has no appreciation for Amelia's condescending tone.

"Inconvenient? As lung cancer!" Trey retorted.

Amelia spun around on her heels and left Trey standing in the hallway. He called out to her as she walked away, "A pleasure, as always."

He walked back into Amelia's private office and mumbled under his breath. "And by 'pleasure', I mean 'pain in the ass'!"

CHAPTER 3

The only light in the darkened room was a single lamp on a desk. A man sat in an office chair, hunched over and with great attention, worked on an "art" project. Magazine pages were scattered on the desk, along with scissors and glue.

Music played in the background. Sarah Brightman belted out "Think of Me" from "The Phantom of the Opera" soundtrack.

His gloved hand held a pair of tweezers and a scrap of paper with the letter C on it. He held it for a moment and thought of words that began with C that would describe her. Cruel. Controlling. Conceited. Costly. Critical. Crappy. Captive...

He picked up the bottle of glue and squeezed out a drop onto the back of the paper, then added it to the piece.

"That bitch probably won't appreciate the talent I'm putting into her love note," he thought to himself. He infused hatred into every part of the project: every drop of glue, every cut of the scissors, each letter he placed.

The patchwork hate letter read:

WATCH YOUR BACK. KARMA IS A BITC

He picked up an **H** and glued it to the page, then admired his handiwork for a few seconds, blowing on it to dry the glue. He slid the note into a very generic mailing envelope. He used a damp paper towel to moisten the glue and seal the envelope, careful not to leave any traces of himself for the cops to find.

He knew the note was old school but also the safest way to remain anonymous. Even a note sent from a public computer could be traced. Damned technology. Besides, Amelia Melchor would find out soon enough who her true admirer was, but the timing would be on his terms.

CHAPTER 4

Amelia strolled into her office, glad to be back at work. Shutting the doors for the two days it took to repair the damage was more than she could handle. "Take a vacation. Who does he think he is, anyway?" she mumbled to herself as she inspected her surroundings to make sure everything looked perfect for her first appointment of the day.

The law offices of Melchor and Associates was located in the heart of the city in an upscale office area, and their client list included many wealthy and influential members of the community. No expense was spared in making sure it met their expectations and helped to justify her exurbanite hourly rate.

Amelia's office phone buzzed, announcing the arrival of Mrs. Diane Jackson. "Thank you, Karen, send her in."

Mrs. Jackson spent the next half hour explaining how she was a victim of her circumstances and how horrible her marriage had been on her lately.

"How can I be expected to take care of *his* house and *his* kids with everything else I have in my life?" Ms. Jackson queried.

Amelia knew the right words to say, having said them many times before, with customized touches of sympathy in all the right places.

"Mrs. Jackson, Diane, I have to tell you that watching a family come apart is absolutely the hardest part of my job. But I think it's better for the children to grow up in two loving homes than in a single home filled with strife."

Mrs. Jackson teared up and nodded her head in agreement.

Amelia continued, "Sometimes people just fall out of love. That's a terrible fact. You said it right, 'How can you love a man who demands so much of your time and energy?' He can get off his lazy ass and fix his own supper! Pardon my turn of phrase."

Mrs. Jackson continued nodding as tears spilled down her cheeks. Finally someone understood her pain. Amelia slid a box of tissues over to her. It would be a shame to ruin that nice silk blouse.

"You deserve happiness. And I'm going to do my dead level best to soften the blow by making sure you and the children are well provided for." Amelia put her hand on a three inch stack of papers on her desk.

"I have your husband's financial statements, thank you for having copies ready, and I'll be going through them with a fine tooth comb into the early hours of the morning. In the meantime, check into the Double Tree for the night. I'll have your husband served with papers at his office first thing tomorrow morning."

Amelia stood, which prompted her client to stand as well. Amelia shook Ms. Jackson's hand and added, "But don't be away from the house for more than 36 hours. If it appears you've abandoned it, we could lose it in the settlement. Your husband will appreciate what it takes to handle the children when he's left with them tonight..."

Amelia sat back in her chair and buzzed her secretary as Ms. Jackson exited her office. Karen... let's go ahead and get Mrs. Jackson's retainer in the bank right away. I want papers ready for her husband before we leave the office tonight. Great. Thanks."

She smiled as she leaned back in her chair, proud of her morning's acquisition. Another day, another divorce, another fee.

~~~~~~

A pair of hands wearing black leather gloves laid a dozen very dried and dead long-stem roses into a long white gift box. The mystery man placed a small envelope on top of the stems, then carefully put a large red bow around the "gift". The large man's hands then set the box aside for future delivery.

CHAPTER 5

Amelia strolled into her office, talking to someone on her Bluetooth cellphone connection. Her secretary, Karen, attempted to speak to her, but was met with Amelia's upheld finger, signaling her to "wait a sec" and breezed right past her.

As she opened the door to her private office, she ran smack into Detective Johnson, who was exiting at the same time. Their collision caused her to drop her attaché. "Aaahhh!" she shrieked.

"Whoa, easy...." Trey clutched onto her arms and helped steady her.

Amelia jerked herself away from him, and spoke into her headset, "Sorry Mrs. Jackson, someone startled me... No, I'm fine. Let me call you right back in a few, Okay? And make sure to enjoy a nice, healthy breakfast! Room service offers an amazing Eggs Benedict with all the trimmings. Thank you. B-bye now." She ended her call and turned to Trey.

"What are you doing in my office?" Her tone was angry. "Do you have a warrant? Karen, did you let him in here?" Heads were going to roll.

Karen didn't answer but swiftly answered the ringing office phone. Saved by the bell.

Trey took the defense, "Hey, stifle yourself, lady. Whether or not you realize it, you need me right now."

Amelia cocked an eyebrow at him, "Need you… here? I don't need anyone, least of all you, Detective! Haven't I made that abundantly clear by now?"

Trey was stone-faced, "Don't flatter yourself." He motioned over his shoulder to Amelia's desk. "Your fan club is at it again. Karen called it in."

Amelia tried her best to remain stoic, but the gasp she let out as she looked at the items on her desk gave her away. Only for a moment…

"Crime Scene has already come and gone. No prints, no fibers."

She stepped closer. The dead roses, along with the patchwork hate letter were laid out across her desk.

"You're welcome," Trey stated.

Amelia ignored his sarcasm she leaned in for a closer look.

"My personal favorite is the 'Roses are dead…' poem. Kind of a twist on a classic." Trey took a little too much pleasure in that jab.

He was grating on her nerves, which helped turn any fear into extreme annoyance. "Detective, while I appreciate your concern. These guys are obviously cowards, otherwise they'd face me rather than hide behind this foolishness."

"Ms. Melchor, they are not voting to make you Miss Congeniality here. These are threats against an officer of the court. Now, I'm giving you notice that I'm calling the FBI in on this one before one of your 'cowards' gets his courage up and decides to escalate his activities."

"Detective, I assure you that won't be necessary. I look at this as a badge of honor, telling me I'm doing my job, separating innocent women from the brutality of their everyday lives."

"You can deflect with a political speech if you want, but.."

She cut him off, "I've been getting these little warnings for the past five years of my practice. But you and I both know that they are empty threats at best."

"Amelia..."

"Detective... my practice can ill afford the type of press that would accompany an FBI investigation. Then what happens to the pro bono work we do for low income families and women in need? What happens to them, Detective? Last time I looked there wasn't a line of attorneys at the courts waiting to take their cases."

"That pious attitude is going to get you into trouble." It was the detective's turn to be annoyed. "Pride comes before a fall, Ms. Melchor."

"Look... I appreciate the gesture, but I'm fine. I'm very careful, I keep my doors locked and I have *Arnold*." She reached into her purse and pulled out *Arnold*, a ladies' hammerless .38 caliber revolver.

"Okay Ms. Melchor, okay. We'll play it your way, as usual. But if these incidents continue to escalate, I'm making the call. No argument." He raised his hands in surrender, knowing personally how stubborn she was.

Amelia tried to smile but the best she could do was smirk. With a tilted head she replied. "I'll personally hand you the phone. Thank you, Detective."

Detective Johnson gathered up Amelia's "gift" in his Latex-gloved hands. "I'll need to take these into evidence. Maybe there's something else the lab can do." He picked up the notes and the flowers and headed to the door.

As he walked out of her office, he casually mentioned over his shoulder, "You know... statistically you're more likely to be killed by that thing than you are to actually defend yourself."

"So I've been told," she answered. "Thank you for stopping by, " she said, not caring whether he could hear her or not.

Amelia slowly sat down behind her desk. She picked up a dead leaf that had fallen out of the box. She twirled it in between her fingers and then threw it in the trash can. She picked up her office phone and dialed three digits. "Karen, get my sister on the phone... well then look it up, she's in the book."

Amelia replaced the receiver and sat back in her chair as she waited for her phone call. Her face donned a thousand mile stare into an uncertain future.

CHAPTER 6

Angela sat quietly at the table as she watched her sister look over the bill for their expensive meal, like some crusty old accountant. She sipped her after-dinner coffee as she glanced outside at the beautifully lit Christmas decorations. The restaurant was elegant and sophisticated; the food was prepared by one of the finest chefs in the city.

Yet as lovely as the atmosphere was, neither lady looked comfortable. Though they sat at a small table for two, there was an invisible chasm of tension between the siblings.

Amelia laid the bill on the table, leaned back and asked, "So, how are my nephews?"

"Kevin is taking Karate now. He's all boy. We're hoping martial arts will teach him discipline. Kris is doing well in school; he loves reading, like his aunt Amelia."

Amelia's laugh interrupted her. It was forced and fake. "Uh, be careful with that one. I don't think this family could survive another attorney in the ranks."

Angela knew her sister all too well. The nice restaurant, the forced small talk. "Amelia, what do you want?" Her tone was flat and direct. The tension increased.

Amelia cracked another fake smile and replied, "What are you talking...

Angela cut her off, "You haven't returned any of my calls lately. We haven't heard from you in months. It's like you don't even have a family anymore. And now I'm in this fancy restaurant answering questions about nephews you haven't laid eyes on in over two years. That's what I'm talking about."

Amelia stared at her without defending or apologizing. The chasm grew.

Angela continued, "So what's going on? Are you dying? Are you in some kind of trouble?"

"Why do you assume it's about me, Ang? Can't I just see my big sister without being cross examined?"

"Not since you passed the bar. The last time we had one of these was when Davis walked out on you. The time before that was the first time you caught him cheating... I may only be a CPA, but I recognize a trend."

Amelia deflected the harsh comments with the usual passive-aggressive onslaught. "I'm sorry you feel that way, Ang. I guess I was wrong. I'm sorry I bothered you... you can go, I'll get the check." She waived her hand back and forth for effect.

This was familiar territory. Angela was not giving up that easy. "Amelia Anne. The same mother raised us both. It's not like you weren't going to pay the bill anyway. Put away the guilt trip and tell me what's on your mind."

Amelia blurted it out, "I'm running for judge."

Angela was taken completely by surprise. "What? That's what this is about? What kind of judge?"

"Family Court," Amelia replied, quite proud of herself.

"That's good Meeli, I hope that does it for you."

"Does what for me?... What?"

"Give you the sense of empowerment and control you need in your life!" At this point, Angela wasn't going to hold back. Amelia was a deer in the headlights. This level of honesty from her sister was new to her.

"We all know what he did to you. He embarrassed you in front of your friends and family. He slept with everything in a skirt and blamed it on you for not 'being there'. What was it he called it, 'emotionally bankrupt?' And then to add insult to injury, he rubbed elbows with the Judge and walked away with everything, including your self-respect."

While Angela talked, Amelia's attention drifted away to another area of the restaurant. It then drifted to another time.

~~~~~~~

At a cozy table for two sat Amelia and her husband, Davis. This had been Amelia's favorite restaurant before Davis came along. When she was new in his law practice, Amelia had taken many a prospective client here to wine and dine.

It was also her favorite personal retreat where she could enjoy a nice glass of Cabernet with something "off the menu" from Executive Chef Milo. Now that she was married, Amelia happily added Davis to the equation. However, that bliss was short-lived.

On this particular night, the couple enjoyed cocktails and appetizers while awaiting their entrees when Davis received a most inconvenient surprise. A very attractive passerby offered greetings.

"Davis?" The elegant beauty queried, "What are you doing here?"

Davis tried to play it off, but he was a deer in the headlights. He quickly threw his napkin from his lap to the table and stood up like a human curtain between to two women. "Jessica..." The attractive interloper leaned in to kiss Davis, which he maneuvered into a clumsy hug.

Confident in her marriage, Amelia sat back and waited to be introduced. She glanced at the woman, then at her husband wearing a polite smile. Unfortunately, the well-dressed young woman was just as confident.

She reached around Davis and courteously extended her hand to Amelia. "Who's your friend, Davis?"

Davis looked sucker-punched; Amelia was. When she realized what was taking place in this very crowded restaurant, Amelia stood to her feet.

"I'm Amelia, Davis's wife." She firmly grabbed the extended hand of the other woman and shook it vigorously. Jessica's mouth fell open. She immediately turned to Davis.

"Did she just say 'wife'?"

Davis opened his mouth but nothing of value came out. "Let me explain…" was all he could utter. In an attempt to help him expand his vocabulary, Jessica grabbed his beverage from the table and threw it in Davis' face. It was a full glass so there was considerable collateral damage.

"You're a pig! How's that for an explanation?" Jessica turned to Amelia, "I'm so sorry!" Jessica stormed out of the restaurant leaving a wake of wet, disgruntled patrons and a mortified Amelia.

Amelia looked at the chaos around her, then her attention turned to her dripping husband. "What are you looking at?" was all he had to say. Shamed before many of their friends and acquaintances, her husband then stomped in the direction of the Men's room.

Amelia was left standing there embarrassed, surrounded by angry patrons whose high priced dining experience had been ruined. This would cost her more than money. Her humiliation festered into fury.

~~~~~~~

"Stay in your lane, Angela." Amelia was getting angry; after all, she did not know how to deal with legitimate concern. Amelia could not even process it, much less acknowledge it. She looked around the restaurant to make sure no one noticed their conversation. Not the kind of behavior befitting a Judge. She wanted to cry, but pulled the emotion back.

Angela continued, "You were so low we were really worried about you. Then you jump from criminal to family law and punish every husband like he's Davis made over. Not that some of them didn't deserve it, I'm sure. We keep reaching out but it's radio silence with you! Mom and I finally figured we had to let you deal with it your way, in your time."

Angela saw that her words weren't reaching her sister. She softened her tone and reached for Amelia's hand on the table. "Meeli, give it everything you've got, and I really hope this brings you back to yourself. Because we love you and we miss you." She slowly, yet deliberately pulled her hand back, stood, grabbed her purse from where it hung on the back of her chair and walked away.

When Angela was out the door, Amelia quietly revealed herself. "Oh and by the way, I got two new death threats today. So how was *your* day?"

She was alone again. Fighting her emotions, she handed the waiter her credit card to pay the bill.

CHAPTER 7

Judge Haney let out a long sigh as he shuffled the papers in front of him. To the casual observer, it would appear he didn't care to be in court that day. Before him stood a divorced couple and their attorneys; Amelia Melchor was there to represent the ex-wife.

He spoke to his clerk without lifting his head, "Okay, Michelle. What do we have here?"

"Your Honor, we have Casem v Casem in the matter of a child support increase request," Michelle replied.

"Ms. Melchor? Why are we here again? I granted your client's prior increase. Not enough cost of living adjustment?" His tone expressed how annoyed he was to have to revisit the issue.

"Yes you did, Your Honor, and your petitioner is most grateful. But it has come to our attention that Mister Casem has come into a sizable inheritance that he is squandering on his latest indiscretion."

"Objection, Your Honor." The opposing attorney, Mr. Manning, blurted. The term 'indiscretion' is clearly inflammatory! Mister Casem is a divorced man and as such can visit socially with whomever he chooses."

"Your Honor, Mister Casem's conduct is what's inflammatory here! His 'social' interludes with Miss... Webster is it... have grown from the occasional "afternoon delight" to overnight stays in Mister Casem's home, even on visitation days."

Amelia continued, her tone indignant, "I believe you can clearly see from this surveillance photo that Mister Casem is having intercourse with a young woman old enough to be Tiffany's older sister!" she waved a photo in the air as she spoke.

Mr. Casem fervently whispered in his attorney's ear. His index finger pounded on the desk in anger. His face was beet red.

Judge Haney perked up. "You have photos of intercourse, Ms. Melchor?"

"Social intercourse, Your Honor. Or is that discourse?" she taunted. "Well, see for yourself." She held out the photos as the bailiff walked in her direction.

Mr. Manning was on it. "Objection your honor! I fail to see the relevance here. There's no way she has photos of a sexual nature. I move to exclude those images from these proceedings!" The bailiff stopped in his tracks and waited for instructions from the Judge.

Judge Haney looked over his glasses as he spoke, "I'm sure you do. Ms. Melchor, care to respond?"

"Your Honor, I think these pictures are worth a thousand words. They're self-explanatory, but I will let your honor make that determination."

She held the photos out to the bailiff once again. Mister Casem grabbed his attorney by his suit jacket and pulled him downward for a chat.

The bailiff prepared to take them from Amelia when Mr. Manning interrupted. "Your Honor, my client has no problem granting the additional child support to his ex-wife. He feels it is in the best interest of his children."

Judge Haney replied, "Yes, I'm quite sure. Draw up the agreement and this court will sign it." The Judge picked up his gavel and thwack, done deal. "Next case, Michelle."

As the parties left the courtroom, Mr. Casem looked at Amelia as if he could strangle her. Once they were in the hallway, Mr. Manning turned to Amelia. "You'll get your papers; I want the pictures."

Amelia snapped back while her client gloated. "Are you stupid? The Judge said I get my papers and if you have any doubts about that we can turn right back around and dance a little more; but its seems to me your client has two left feet." Manning and Casem glared at her.

Amelia continued to pile it on, "And I think I'll hold on to the pictures. I've got quite a collection going, and I'd hate to break up the set."

Mr. Manning spoke between clenched teeth, "I realize you're not here to make friends, but every dog has his day! In your case, her day!" He pulled Mr. Casem by the arm and left the courthouse. Manning scolded his client on the way out. "Try keeping that thing in your pants and maybe you can retire one day!"

CHAPTER 8

Late in the evening, after court, Amelia was working at her office. She was typing away on her computer when a knock on the door startled her. She jumped in her chair and clutched her chest. "Holy crap, Karen!"

"I'm sorry, Boss. I didn't mean to startle you," Karen apologized.

"It's ok. I was just very focused. I forgot you were here," Amelia replied.

"I've got today's mail, along with a couple of special deliveries." Karen plopped the stack onto Amelia's desk.

"Excellent. Hopefully one of them is Mr. Casem's judgement."

"Hope so. Well if that's all, I'm going to call it a day," Karen replied.

"Good night, see you in the morning," Amelia eyed the stack of mail as she waived her off. She heard Karen gather her things and shut and lock the outer office door. She picked up an envelope marked "special delivery" and ripped it open. "Come on sweet payday!"

No luck, it was just a notice from another attorney. Amelia opened another one and pulled out the contents, anticipating the news. She read the hand-written note:

"Sorry I missed you the other night. But I do look forward to catching up with you real soon."

When Amelia realized who the note was from, chills ran through her entire body. She sat frozen in fear. BAM, BAM, BAM. Loud knocking on her front door. "Aaaahhh!" she shrieked, nearly jumping out of her skin.

She shouted to the would be intruder, "Go away! I'm calling the police!" she scrambled for her phone and opened it.

She heard a voice yell through the door, "I AM the police!"

Amelia's heart was pounding. Did she hear that correctly? "Detective?" she asked, her hand ready to dial 911.

"No. I'm a serial killer. I just thought I'd be polite and knock first." He enjoyed toying with her.

Amelia shoved the note back into the envelope and jammed it into her desk drawer. She nervously quipped back, "Well give me a minute to empty my purse while looking for that useless handgun and I'll be right with you." She started for the door to let him inside and hoped he wouldn't read the fear on her.

The Detective tapped his fingers on the glass as he waited for her to open the door. He was not known for his patience.

She unlatched the deadbolt and slowly opened the door to allow him in. "It's after business hours, Detective. To what do I owe the pleasure?"

His face was stern, and his tone was no longer jovial. "I came by to let you know that our lab has determined that you're looking at at least four perps in the destruction of your property. That's gotta be a record."

"Only four?" She asked, as she deliberately sat on the couch in the waiting area. He stood over her, which she noted as his tactic to have control.

"My thoughts exactly. I figured you were looking at six or more. But time will tell."

"Let me ask you something, do you have this much fun at the expense of all your cases, or does that privilege belong to me alone?"

"Ms. Melchor, you are pretty much my entire case load right now, a little tidbit that's become quite an annoyance because you aren't takin' this thing as seriously as I think it truly is. Have I mentioned that at least four people out there mean you some kind of harm?"

"So why add to your grief by coming downtown to tell me this in person when you could have disparaged me over the phone and saved yourself a trip? ...I'm sure you're not looking for my legal advice on a particular matter."

He remained standing over her, and it took everything she had to stay seated. "As a matter of fact, I got an overtime allowance from the chief. I also have an extra rotation for a couple of black and whites to patrol this area. You're welcome."

Amelia knew she had no reason to object to that, so she said nothing as he continued. It wasn't easy for her to show gratitude.

"Perhaps a show of force, a little added police presence will take this thing down a notch or two." Trey got personal, "We absolutely have our differences, you and me. But it is my professional opinion that your safety is in jeopardy, perhaps even your life. And nothing is worth that. No silly notion of principal, not bravado, not pride and certainly not our history."

"Differences? We have our differences? This sudden display of care and concern is touching, but hardly necessary..." that was as close to a thank you he was going to get from her tonight.

"Good night, Ms. Melchor. Careful on your way home." Trey started toward the door and Amelia followed to see him out. He hoped his attempt to appear detached was believable. He opened the door and stepped across the threshold.

"Also, You know, you should change out that hand latch for a keyed deadbolt. If they break out the glass, they just have to reach in and unlock it themselves," Trey stated matter-of-factly.

"It's a glass door, Detective. If they break out the glass, they don't need to unlock it. Good thing it's not you locking my doors at night." She briefly thought of a time when it was... She quickly added, "Good night, Detective."

He waived over his shoulder as he turned and headed to his car.

CHAPTER 9

The Rosewick Hotel was buzzing with excitement; the night ahead was to be an elegant affair. Anyone who was anyone was in attendance, and the crowd that gathered were there for one reason, a news-worthy announcement.

Amelia arrived, stepped out of her BMW, and handed the keys to the valet before walking to the hotel entrance. She was dressed in an elegant evening gown, her hair coifed to perfection, and everything about her appearance was flawless.

As she headed up the steps, she suddenly felt unnerved. A car crept slowly by, and she felt more uneasy. She decided to confront the automobile with a glance. Her mood quickly turned to annoyance as she spotted Trey in his unmarked car. She huffed and picked up the pace to get inside.

Christmas trees with twinkling white lights adorned the halls and the ballroom was absolutely splendid. The flower-sprayed tables were dressed in the finest linens and topped with delicious hors d'oeuvres. The wait staff in black bow ties and matching vests made sure that every guest had a glass of wine or a cocktail, offered up on polished trays.

The room was abuzz with small talk, given the reason for the gathering. A tink-tink-tink on a wine glass drew their attention to the host, as he took his place behind the podium and adjusted the microphone. "Ladies and gentlemen," he announced to gain the attention of the guests.

The crowd began to quiet as he continued, "Ladies and gentlemen, welcome one and all. Welcome friends for better government. I'm Chip Ourso, serving City Council District 13 and your host for this evening." A light applause filled the room, and Mr. Ourso nodded his thanks to them.

"I know many of you would agree that there are so many things that are 'right' with our city. Wages are up, our splendid downtown is experiencing quite a renaissance, and thanks to the generosity of the Shanks family, we have a new arts center pouring its foundation on Monday."

The crowd offered a cordial "golf clap" that rose and fell like a single heartbeat.

"But we would be less than honest if we didn't recognize that we must effect change at certain levels of government if we are going to reach our full potential." Nods of agreement were sprinkled throughout the audience.

"There are those of us who believe that our families are under attack... from the place we'd least expect: our family courts." More nods and a few claps echoed in the room.

"Without that family unit, that most basic foundation, I and several of my colleagues imagine that we'd weaken the fabric of our fair city and jeopardize our bright future."

Again the guests offered an approving golf clap.

"And it is to that end that these colleagues, a collective of city policymakers have asked one very brave woman to take on the challenge of delivering justice to our families." The excitement of the attendees was growing; murmurs and whispers filled the room.

"Ladies and gentlemen, I present to you our next Family Court Judge, Amelia Melchor!" The crowd erupted into applause, as Amelia took her place at the microphone. She graciously bowed and flashed her million dollar smile. She stood there for a few moments, acknowledging and absorbing the adulation.

"Thank you... thank you so much," she began. She glanced at the 3x5 cards now in her hands. "How could anyone follow an introduction like that?" She smiled again as her audience laughed softly. She really had the "perfect candidate" routine down pat.

"Someone... " Amelia shot a glance referring to Councilman Ourso, "asked me, 'Why would a successful attorney with a thriving practice take on such a tremendous responsibility, a seat on the family court bench, not to mention a serious cut in pay?'" More soft laughter.

"Why indeed?" she paused for effect, "Because sometimes it's more important to do what is right than what is comfortable." She had them right where she wanted them; church had begun. The first vote had not been cast, but Amelia held court right then and there.

"Sometimes it is better to do what is most charitable, if you understand the full meaning of that word, rather than what is most profitable. I've dedicated my law practice to the service of the family, that foundational unit that Councilman Ourso spoke of so eloquently."

Amelia surveyed the crowd and realized there were faces she didn't recognize. "The families of our city are suffering.." One man in particular was staring a hole right through her, succeeding in unnerving her.

"Suffering from a disease called apathy." A few moments later, the man was joined by his date and they walked off, all smiles. False alarm.

"The same judges seated in the same position, year after year." Amelia locked eyes with another man. "I know this because I stand before these judicial artifacts every day. I believe it's time for some new blood." She looked down at her cards, looked back, and he was gone.

"I think our families deserve better." Amelia spotted a flower arrangement on the buffet table.

"I think our families deserve someone who will dedicate themselves to justice." The next time she looked up from her speech, flowers suddenly appeared dead like the flowers that she received the day before.

"Someone who will be fair and open-minded." She looked back at the arrangement and they were just fine, as they were before.

Amelia hoped no one noticed that little beads of sweat were forming on her forehead. "Someone who will be fair... and open minded. Someone who will put the best interests of our children above the petty bickering of their parents."

She glanced down at her note cards and saw the hate note instead of her speech. "Sorry I missed you the other night..." Her world began to spin.

She squeezed her eyes shut for a moment. "I hope you will give me a chance to be that person..." She opened her eyes and saw the correct concluding remark, "...on election day! Thank you!"

The crowd cheered loudly, and their applause was now deafening. She stepped away from the podium as the crowd surrounded her, congratulating and celebrating. She felt overwhelmed at the sudden rush of attention and wished she could push them all away and flee the room. That was not what a "good candidate" would do. She needed their support, their money.

Mr. Ourso was back at the microphone and announced, "Ladies and gentlemen, your next Family Court Judge... Ms. Amelia Melchor. Tonight we're asking for your financial support to help put her..."

Amelia didn't hear the rest of the speech. She was swept away by the horde of people pushing against her. She glared at every face wondering which one could be "him" or even "them". Even though she felt smothered, Amelia answered as many questions as she could before retiring to the hotel lounge for a much needed drink.

CHAPTER 10

The hotel lounge was the perfect hideaway for Amelia. She sat at the bar, nursing a cocktail, and stared into it as though the answer to every question was in the bottom of the glass. But there was nothing but a plain white napkin there, moistened by the sweating glass. At least the alcohol had calmed her nerves a bit.

Her escape was short lived. "Ms. Melchor?" The voice slightly startled and annoyed her at the same time. She spun her barstool in the general direction of a man and a woman whom she recognized from the earlier fund raiser. Amelia instantly went into "good candidate" mode and smiled at them, pretending to give them her full attention.

"I didn't get the chance to visit with you one on one earlier... not one to fight crowds. But I just want you to know that we appreciate everything you said and we take it to heart."

Amelia extended her hand and replied, "Thank you, Mister..."

"Aldridge. Evan Aldridge. This is my wife, Sydney. And you're very welcome."

Amelia spun her bar stool and her attention back to her drink on the bar.

Evan, emboldened by the amount of his forthcoming "donation", was oblivious to Amelia's social cue. "So what do you think would be your first order of business when you get into office?"

She shot back, "Fire my clerk." The "candidate smile" on Amelia's face somehow turned her blatant sarcasm into an eccentric sense of humor.

Evan stood there, blinked back confusion, then replied with a smile, "Oh... that's a joke, isn't it?"

"Yessir it is... There's so much to be done Mr. Aldridge, I'm not sure where I'd start. But I promise it will be somewhere." Amelia reassured him with a "good ole boy" wink.

The hint was sinking in, and Evan's tone was apologetic, "Well, we'll bid you goodnight, Ms. Melchor. And we're pulling for you. We'll be leaving our contribution with Daryl."

"That means so much. Good night, to you both." Her best candidate smile was once more forced upon her unwilling face, and she waived them back into the ballroom.

Amelia reached for her glass without looking at it and took a long draw on her drink. It went down smooth. She turned and placed the drink back on the napkin and twirled the stir straw around the small amount of liquid left in the glass.

As Amelia returned to her search for answers at the bottom of her glass, she found a truth that made her skin crawl. Her heart pounded so loud that it drowned out the rest of the room as she lifted her beverage. "Tonight's the Night!" had been handwritten in red ink on the sweaty napkin.

This time it was not her imagination; in fact it was too real. Her first instinct was to examine the drink. Was she poisoned? One terrifying fact, the perpetrator was close. Maybe he had brushed up against her and she hadn't even noticed, being distracted by her supporters. Were the Aldridges in on it?

Amelia quickly slammed the glass down on the bar and wiped her mouth with her hand. Trying not to appear panicked, her head was on a swivel as she reached into her purse and threw a few dollars on the bar top.

She stood, took a quick glance around and scurried for the exit. Amelia kept her head down, not wanting to draw attention to herself or let on to the fact that she was more frightened than she had ever been in her life to this moment. She couldn't walk fast enough and didn't breathe until she burst through the front door of the Rosewick.

CHAPTER 11

Amelia rushed to the valet stand, which was unoccupied. "Shit!" she mumbled under her breath. She needed to go and it had to be now! She looked around for the attendant, thinking he might show up at any moment, but he was nowhere in sight.

Unnerved, she frantically searched for her key in the valet's unlocked cabinet. Finding it among the barrage of luxury car keys, she snatched it off the hook and raced toward the valet parking area in the adjacent lot.

She took a quick look over her shoulder and let out a sigh of relief that she wasn't being followed. WHAM! She ran headlong into a large man. "Aahhh!" she yelped.

The man reached for her elbow to steady her. "Whoa, beautiful. No need to be in a rush. Why don't you step inside and let me get you something to calm your nerves?"

Amelia was in no mood to be patronized. She tried to jerk her arm away from the man. "Get off me!" she sneered at him. The smell of alcohol wafted through the air.

"Wow! I think maybe you've had *too* much to drink, darlin'. You'd better come back in and let me call you a cab." He now had both hands on her as she was fighting to pull away from him, but he was too big and strong. She would have to outwit him.

"I said get off of me!" she jerked her arm again and began to scream, "Fire, fire!" The man immediately let go of her and Amelia continued her high-heeled trek to the safety of her car.

"If you're hell bent on dying tonight, lady, I'm not getting in your way," the massive man barked after her. Little did he know his choice of words were almost prophetic. As Amelia disappeared into the darkness, he turned back toward the Rosewick and his appointment with Mr. Jack Daniels.

Amelia pressed the locator button on her keys and ran toward her car as it sounded off, looking over her shoulder to make sure she wasn't followed.

She arrived at her vehicle, popped the lock, swooped inside and locked the doors. Safe behind the wheel, she let out a long sigh. Amelia then began to second guess herself. Had she over-reacted? Was the note from one of her stalkers or encouragement from a well-meaning donor?

She clutched the steering wheel and laid her head on her hands. Safe. She looked up and glanced around the parking lot, then sat back in the seat for a few moments to gather herself.

Amelia leaned forward and put the key in the ignition. She turned it over and the stereo blasted Garth Brooks, "*I've Got Friends in Low Place*," startling her once again. She instinctively reached for the volume knob and brought the sound level down, along with her heart rate. Another deep breath and she reached for the rear view mirror. She tilted it down to check her makeup, then back in place. No one hiding in the back seat.

Amelia then addressed her rear view and began backing out of her parking space. She uttered her familiar mantra, "This is ridiculous. This is nothing you can't..." BAM! A car came out of nowhere, and Amelia hit it squarely. That crossed her last nerve!

Amelia stepped out of the car and immediately scrutinized the damage to her BMW. Fear gave way to anger. "Are you kidding me?! You'd better have some serious insurance! What kind of..." She craned her neck and squinted her eyes to inspect the damage in the dim light of the parking lot.

"This is unbelievable!" She screeched. Pieces of tail light were scattered on the ground. "Oh no... you've stepped in it now buddy. You just..." Her agitation and a modest amount of alcohol left her somewhat speechless. She grabbed her cell phone from her car. The driver of the other vehicle now exited his car.

"Do you have any idea who I..." her voice trailed off as she turned to face the other driver and was met with a fist coming straight at her face. Blackness.

CHAPTER 12

"So the accuser is now the accused!" the man's voice boomed in Amelia's ears. She opened her eyes, still dazed from the blow to her head. Her eyes adjusted to the dim lighting enough to recognize that she was in a court room. The only light was provided by a few recessed, incandescent lights scattered in the drop ceiling that created small pools of illumination.

She wanted to reach for her aching head, but she was unable. As she grew more lucid, she became aware of the fact that her arms were bound with duct tape. She was restrained in the witness chair.

"Glad you could join us, counselor. Did you enjoy your nap?" The voice, filled with sarcastic disdain, was closer now.

Amelia came to herself, "Help me! Fire! Fire! Anyone!" Amelia screamed at the top of her lungs in full survival mode.

The menace, the source of her deepest nightmare, was suddenly right in front of her. He mocked her useless pleas, "Help me, oh somebody help me! Fire! Fire! Which one are you, Beavis or Butthead?"

Amelia could feel his breath on the nape of her neck but held her resolve. She jerked at the bindings, to no avail. "Fight all you want; scream your lungs out, counselor; it won't do you any good. No one can hear you in here, and no one is coming for you," the voice taunted.

She struggled to free herself anyway. Her fight was less than fruitful.

"I'll do you the courtesy of this one suggestion... save your strength -- you're gonna need it." The voice disappeared into the darkness again. His campaign of terror had begun.

"You're messing with the wrong bitch. Do you have any idea who I am? I have important friends in this town..."

"You're overplaying your hand, counselor. Since you already know who I am, I have a better question. 'Do you know what I'm capable of?'" He circled around her like a lion sizing up its prey.

Amelia was shaken but defiant. "You mean the psychopath that's been sending me all this childish hate mail? Coward! I'm no therapist, but I'm fairly sure that you're expressing a certain lack in other departments!"

His laughter from the darkness was jarring, but Amelia was relentless. "So if you've got something in mind, dickless, then let's get on with it! But I'm fairly certain you don't have the stones for it, so save us both some time and cut me loose."

Silence. Amelia strained to see where he was. Did he leave? "Well?" she quizzed him.

Clap! Clap! Amelia jumped at the loud, solitary hand claps that came from the darkness behind her. He moved around her and stopped under one of the recessed lighting units in the gallery, and she looked him squarely in the face.

"My, counselor, what an inflated sense of self-importance you still have. I thought some of my trinkets would have taken that attitude down a notch or two," he taunted her.

She glared back at him, his words ringing in her ears.

"No worries," he said. "Makes my job here that much easier. Sloppy diagnosis as to who I am though. Not surprising. I am who you made me." He then moved out of the light in the direction of the prosecution's desk.

Amelia replied, "I'm assuming you're an ex of one of my clients. What you're doing is illeg…" she stopped short when he held up her purse that had rested on the desk.

"I have discovery to present to the witness." He stated dryly.

"That's my purse!" She shouted back at him.

He dumped the contents onto the desk. Its contents came tumbling out with quite a racket, aggressively piercing the darkness.

"If it's money you're after, just take it. You don't need me here for that!" Amelia stated as a matter of fact.

"If I may proceed," he said, as he rummaged through her possessions. He spread them out on the table: a compact, lipstick, a wallet, keys on a keyring, and a revolver were among the items.

"Leave my things alone!" she snarled at him. She hated that she let her emotions escape her mouth unchecked.

"I'll take whatever I want, counselor, with or without your permission." He pushed around her lipstick, which rolled off the table and onto the floor. He reached toward her pistol but picked up her wallet instead. "Louis Vuitton. Very nice...."

Although Amelia was helpless, she was growing more agitated at the intrusion. She dreaded that helplessness. It was a familiar feeling from her past that she'd thought was long buried.

He opened her wallet, removed her license and looked it over. "Nice picture, counselor. Better hope this isn't the one they post for your obituary." He continued his review, "13245 Willow Road... been there, not impressed. Great neighborhood but the whole 'gated community' thing is a joke. It's interesting how much crap blood money can buy!"

"Character assassination been 'berry, berry good' to you!" He continued in musings interesting only to himself.

"Is *that* what this is about, pick on a defenseless woman who's half your size? What a big man you are! A legend in your own mind," Amelia jabbed. "I guess a rat can squeeze in about anywhere."

He reacted to her sarcasm by charging at her, and the anger in his eyes frightened her. His large frame loomed over her as he straddled her. She froze as he slid his hands under her blouse, tearing it in a show of utter control. She realized at that moment that this wasn't going to end well.

"Defenseless!?! I have a lot of adjectives to describe you, counselor. Defenseless isn't on the list!" Each time he breathed the word "counselor" it wreaked of disgust. His diatribe continued, "Defenseless is having your entire life laid bare in open court in retaliation for trying to do the right thing!"

Amelia sat, motionless and quiet and listened to his rant. She was inundated with fear, but she was not going to give him the satisfaction of seeing it.

"Defenseless... defenseless is an innocent life lost because an illegitimate court order robs you of... everything!" He was done for the moment and moved off of her and back over to the prosecutor's table.

Amelia was dumbfounded by his campaign of shock and awe. Her mind was racing. What could she say to get out of this alive? If he had a weak spot, she would find it. A torn blouse and a bump on the head were pawns in this chess game she was willing to sacrifice to take the king. Unfortunately for her, this was not a game.

"Look, I don't know who you are, and whatever you think I've done to you, I'm sorry. But I'm just a hired hand, just doing my job. Please don't hurt me." She hoped she sounded sincere.

The man picked up her wallet again. "I'm calling bullshit on this 'just doing my job' business. You spin more fiction than J.K. Rowling, woman."

Amelia replied, "In defense of my client..."

"Your client didn't need defending, counselor; she needed help." He continued looking through her wallet. "What was her name, counselor? This client who needed defending?"

"Why do you..."

"Answer the question! You were quick to say she needed "defending". What was her name, this defenseless client?" he queried.

"What does it matter?" Amelia was stalling.

The man made a noise like a penalty buzzer. "Annnnnn. Facts not in evidence! More fiction, counselor. Objection overruled!"

He pulled her credit cards out and flung them across the room like 52 card pick up. "Nordstrom's. Macy's. Bloomingdales. Tiffany's. Oscar de la Renta. Louis Vuitton. Saks Fifth Avenue. Neiman Marcus. Trying to satiate your guilt with material possessions? How's that working out for you, counselor?"

Amelia held her tongue. It was rhetorical anyway.

"No? Ok, well I'm going to go with hedonist on this one then." Once he tossed the last credit card, he reached in and pulled out a business card and held it up. "Now we've hit the motherlode!" He closely scrutinized her card. "Amelia D. Melchor, Attorney at Law! Is this you? The real you?" he asked.

Amelia lifted her head. "Yes," she stated.

"Objection!" He yelled, as he charged at her again.

She readied herself for his wrath. Instead of touching her, he leaned in to her, "Ms. Melchor, is it true that your so-called law practice handles divorces almost exclusively?"

Amelia sat quietly as she contemplated her answer. She knew that no matter what she said, it would be the wrong answer.

He prompted her, "The witness will answer the question!"

She began with, "Most of my clients..."

"Yes or No," he demanded.

"Yes." She answered.

He continued, "And is it true that of these divorce cases, your firm represents women, exclusively, whether plaintiff or defendant?" He reached for the pile on the table, his hand passing over the pistol. Amelia stared at his hand, but he picked up a tampon instead.

"Objection," countered Amelia, "you are attempting to lead the witness." She wouldn't give him the satisfaction of calling him "opposing counsel".

"You're female. Whaddaya know? How fitting..." He discarded the tampon and declared, "Objection, overruled."

Amelia was defiant. "I don't have to answer you."

"You don't ever have to leave this courtroom either... You should know, however, that I've seen your files... all... of your files. And if you refuse to answer, I will be forced to compel you." He moved closer to her. "So is it true, Ms. Melchor?"

Amelia was defensive, "I support women's causes, but I..."

"The witness will answer 'yes' or 'no'."

"No one read me my rights," she replied.

"You have none."

"Then this is a kangaroo court and I don't recognize its authority in this trumped-up case." That was game, set, match in Amelia's mind. If logic and persuasion could have won the day, a mistrial would have been declared, and she would have been a free woman. However, in this case, logic and persuasion were replaced with raw emotion. Amelia remained in her restraints.

The two of them exchanged a hard stare. He continued his taunt with a demented whisper, "Your experience in the real world notwithstanding, in this courtroom, here... now... the punishment for obscuring the facts is instantaneous and will blow your mind."

The man stomped over to the prosecutor's desk and scooped up Arnold, the revolver. He moved in close to Amelia. Light gleaned off the pistol as he popped the cylinder open and emptied the contents into his left hand.

The despot put the pistol's payload on the desk and the .38 caliber bullets rolled freely in every direction. He then picked up a single bullet and held it between the thumb and index finger of his right hand. The dimly lit courtroom obscured Amelia's view, but apparently, the man had placed that single bullet back into the weapon's cylinder.

Her tormentor spun the cylinder around and Amelia could hear the whirring of the steel. "Round and round and round we go..." His scare tactic was having an effect on her, but she remained outwardly stoic.

A flick of his wrist and the cylinder slammed home. Amelia anticipated the worst and knew she needed to act. "You don't have to do this. I'll tell you…"

He banged the grip of the pistol on the Judge's desk five times, as if it were a gavel. Amelia flinched with each bang.

"The witness will not speak unless spoken to."

Amelia looked down, defeated.

"Do you know the term misandrist, counselor?"

She continued staring at the floor and didn't answer.

"Counselor!" He snapped at her, which broke her gaze.

She answered quietly, "It's a woman who hates men."

He pushed her, "Speak up, please! For the record."

Louder, she replied, "It's a woman who hates men."

"That's correct. Would you describe yourself as a misandrist, counselor?" He paced back and forth in front of her, waiting for her answer.

She shook her head no, which angered him. "The witness will answer the question. Are you guilty of misandry?"

She cringed before answering, "I protect women from abusers."

"So in your line of reason, you are protecting your clients because all men are abusers."

"Objection. Relevance?"

"Overruled. The witness will answer."

"I don't understand your question. Why is this relevant? Is this why you've brought me here?" Amelia pressed him as much as she dared.

"I wouldn't want to be accused of leading the witness again. That's more your specialty."

"Fine. I'll answer your question. Just answer me this." Amelia took a dramatic pause, "Who *are* you?"

He laughed and shook his head. She really didn't get it. "What a joke! You just made my entire case for me."

The provoked perpetrator stormed to the prosecutor's desk and grabbed Amelia's business card. He lunged towards her and shoved the card in her face. "Read it! The witness will read the card!"

Amelia tried to focus. She shook her head; sweat was dripping, and she tripped over her words. "It says, it..."

"Read it!"

"Amelia D. Melchor, Attorney at Law," she murmured.

He slammed the card down in front of her, and she flinched. "Attorney at Law! What a misrepresentation of the facts! We have already established that your decision-making process is impaired."

Amelia was torn between defending herself and not wanting to anger her antagonist further. She sat silently while he ranted.

"You don't see the law. You see men whom you hate and an opportunity to profit from your perverse sense of justice. Right… wrong means nothing to you. The men must be punished and the family ripped apart."

Amelia turned her gaze downward once more. His accusations were harsh and unjustified. She had no choice but to sit there while this bully badgered her.

"It makes you feel powerful, doesn't it?" he continued. "For us to sit *there* and you to stand *here* and use your law degree to decide life and death."

"Life and death? Hardly", she thought aloud. She was confused. "I don't try criminal cases anymore."

"Of course not. You've become the criminal."

Amelia's mind was reeling, and she grasped at straws. "Criminal? If that's what you've got, I wasn't Mirandized. I should be released on a technicality."

No way she was getting off that easily. "You have the right to remain silent, but you can't help yourself! And your business card says it right there 'Attorney at Law' so you don't need *one* since you are *one*."

The man stepped closer to her, and although the room was dim, she could see the rage, hatred, and even murder in his eyes. "You want to know who I am?" He got her attention, "I am pain."

She stared at him, too frozen to speak; but her mind couldn't stop. The situation went south quickly. Amelia felt a chill come over her like someone had just stepped over her grave. Her chance to recover any modicum of control passed.

The enraged offender continued his monolog, "I am loss. I am death. I told you, I am who you made me to be. *That's* what brought you here. Only this time I'm the one standing and you're in the seat."

CHAPTER 13

Amelia fought through her fear using reason as a distraction. She needed answers so she could create a better conclusion to her confinement. "What do you want with me?"

The miscreant shoved the gun under Amelia's chin forcing her to look him in the eyes. He cracked a half smile. "I'm afraid that's a loaded question."

Amelia's head was spinning. She wondered if this was going to be her last moment on Earth. Her perpetrator moved around her, she his prey, a caged animal with no escape.

"See, the last time we met, it was *me* with the gun to my head and *your* finger on the trigger."

~~~~~~~

In a well-lit court room in front of a Judge, a jury, and a full gallery, Amelia's captor, apparently, the husband in this case, was seated in the witness seat. His attorney, Verne Clark, stood at the defendant's table.

Amelia was pacing the floor, firing questions at will. "Please tell this court the last time you got into a physical altercation with your wife."

Mr. Clark stood and interjected, "Objection, Your Honor. Facts not in evidence!"

Amelia's assailant pleaded with the Judge from the witness seat, "Your Honor, I never…"

Amelia turned to the Judge, "Permission to treat the witness as hostile." She was the Queen of Chaos. This trial was a three-ring circus, and Amelia was the ringmaster.

The Judge directed his attention to Mr. Clark, "Objection overruled." He then addressed Amelia, "You may proceed."

The witness slumped into the seat, defeated and helpless to plead his case. He glanced at Amelia, who shot him a cocky grin.

~~~~~~~

The memory fortified his feelings of loss and rage. The malicious malefactor stared down at Amelia. He looked her over; she wasn't so cocky now.

Amelia clenched her teeth and mumbled a response, "I don't remember...."

The man yelled at her, "What?"

Amelia repeated, "I don't...."

He jerked the gun up.

"Remember..." she trailed off.

~~~~~~~

Amelia, the representative of the Plaintiff, was in full attack mode, at a near yelling pitch, directed towards the crumbling husband. "And is it true that *you came home late each night because you were involved with your secretary?"*

The husband was adamant, "That's not true, Your Honor."

Amelia was smug, "Your Honor, exhibit A for the Jury please?" On a large screen, indiscreet photos of a man and woman having an affair. The photos were dark, and it was unclear whether or not the man was the defendant.

The witness insisted, "That's not me, Your Honor!"

The Judge spoke to Amelia, "Ms. Melchor, do you have confirmation that these are photos of the defendant?"

"Do we have confirmation that he's a man?" The circus was still in town. Amelia ran a brilliant campaign of confusion and distraction.

Mr. Clark stood to his feet from behind the defendant's table, "Objection Your Honor!"

The Judge slammed his gavel on his desk. "Ms. Melchor, approach the bench."

She walked over and stood in front of the Judge.

The Judge was not as amused as Amelia was. "Ms. Melchor, this court sympathizes that you are going through a very difficult divorce yourself at this time. That said, you will conduct yourself in a professional manner fitting an officer of this court. Step back."

Once again, the Judge ruled in Amelia's favor.

~~~~~~~

Amelia's antagonist grimaced as he stood over her. Amelia's usual over-confidence was nowhere to be seen. She could feel his anger as he spoke, "That's right. You seem to know something about kangaroo courts. But I couldn't help but overhear the Judge's comment concerning your marital demise."

This was troublingly personal and provocative for Amelia.

He kept the pressure on Amelia. "A simple public records request gave me access to every single page of your divorce decree. That was a nasty one. If you were a human being I think I'd almost have to feel sorry for you."

Embarrassed and beleaguered, Amelia fumbled for words. "What..."

"I've read the transcripts. I know everything."

Amelia tried to rationalize. "I can explain... It wasn't personal. I..."

Her kidnapper challenged her, "What was her name?"

Amelia replied, "Her name? Who's name?"

"Here's a hint. She had long hair. Dark. Deep blue eyes. She smelled like roses." He stared into infinity lost in the memory for a few seconds.

Amelia's blank stare angered him. "More? Drinking problem. Five-year-old daughter." His fond memory slipped away into pain.

Amelia said her name, "Marah."

"Ah, there she is," her antagonist stepped back from her, raising his hands in victory, like he had scored a touchdown.

"That would make you… Dave?" Amelia groped for the answer.

"Daniel… Dan," he said, correcting her. "I see you still place a premium on accuracy, counselor."

Amelia saw an opportunity, "As I remember, she was a lovely woman. What would she think of you doing this to me?"

Dan was insulted. "Oh now we worry about how she feels? HOW DARE YOU? You didn't know or care what she needed then; how dare you ask such a question now?"

Amelia observed him and wondered what set him off like that.

Dan quickly recovered. "You know what? Marah's not here. But this is what *I* think about it." He held up the revolver and pointed it at her.

"I understand why you're upset. You lost custody..."

Dan shook his head slowly, his face twisted in disgust. "You have no idea. No idea what my loss is... I wasn't the one in those pictures you presented in court. But *you* know who was!"

Amelia swallowed hard, and her eyes widened. She knew exactly who was in the photos; she just didn't think Dan knew.

He didn't have to spell it out, but he did. "My attorney. You embarrassed him in court, so he signed away my rights. She got full custody. I barely got visitation."

Amelia defended, "Then you should have your attorney disbarred for giving you bad counsel. I was paid to represent my client to the best of my ability. And that's exactly what I did!"

Her response riled him again. He pressed the gun to her head. "LIAR! You didn't represent your client; you didn't give a damn about what she needed! You represented her parents and their huge retainer check. So-called 'justice' bought and paid for."

Dan momentarily lost his lucidity. He pulled back the revolver's hammer. "There's only one bullet in the cylinder. I like your chances."

Dan pulled the trigger. CLICK! The pistol's firing pin struck an empty chamber. Amelia squealed.

"Maybe next time. One can only hope," Dan whispered.

Amelia was frightened to her core, but she tried to keep her composure. Dan stepped back into the darkness. She could hear the sounds of him texting on a phone but didn't dare ask. She was relieved that he was out of sight, if for only a few moments.

CHAPTER 14

Detective Trey Johnson, aka Amelia's emotional punching bag, sat at his desk in the squad room of the 23rd Precinct. He picked up a case file from the modest stack before him and opened it. He looked at the photos inside, spread them out on his desk like puzzle and held a picture of Amelia in his hand. Although it was a professional head shot, it captured her softness. Trey hadn't seen that part of her for quite some time, and he missed it.

Trey's partner, Hank, walked over to his desk and interrupted Trey's concentration. "Grabbing a midnight coffee. You want anything?"

Trey waived his hand back and forth and pointed across the room. "There's a coffee pot right over there."

"That burnt smell? I wouldn't call it coffee... Okay, confession. I need some ice cream." Hank patted his stomach.

Trey smiled and replied, "*I'm* going to call bullshit on that one, but ok. I think you're craving that cute manager lady behind the counter. Better watch it, or you'll get sick from all that heavy cream."

Hank laughed with him and then glanced at the open file on Trey's desk. "Still care, huh?" He gestured to the photo of Amelia.

Trey shrugged and replied, "About my responsibility as a detective, yeah."

"Now I'm the one calling bullshit. You still care about that self-involved, mental case; admit it." Hank picked up her photo.

Trey shot him a look, snatched the photo from Hank and laid it back in the file. "Not in the least. To prove it, I won't take her side and remind you that you're still bitter about the way she handed you your ass in court over the Shomanski case." Hank was not amused. "Wait, what did the guys call you after that…" The partners said unison, "The great white dope."

Trey laughed; Hank, not so much.

"You can give me the stink eye all you want, but you know I'm telling the truth. How long have we been partners?" Hank asked him.

Trey looked at his watch. "About ten minutes too long."

Hank rolled his eyes. "Alright, Superfly, with all this detective work going on, you getting anywhere on this case?"

Trey sighed, "Not really. I can't get her to take it seriously. She won't cooperate, which leaves me exactly nowhere. Waiting on forensics."

Hank knew his partner wasn't being honest with himself. "You're too close to this, you know? Too close to her." He pointed again at her photo.

Trey stared at her photo as Hank continued, "Look at you right now; you care more than she does. Obviously! Face it, she's still the same ole 105 pound sack of crazy you wanted to marry a year ago! A woman whose preferred method of contraception is her personality. She'd rather get shot than actually admit she needs anyone's help. Which easily translates to *one of us* taking a bullet."

"Damn, Hank, why don't you just say what you feel?" Trey realized Hank was right, so he got defensive. "My feelings and our history aside, the woman has a right to our protection, even if it's from herself first and foremost! I just don't want anything to happen to her. Anything, you know, permanent."

Hank wasn't going to let him get off that easily. "That crap right there won't pass the smell test! You'd lose sleep if that girl got a paper cut on her pinky toe. Thing is, if something happens, it's not your problem... she's not your problem. Not anymore. You have more than met your professional responsibility."

Trey looked back at the folder and the photographs. He was agitated because he knew Hank was right. This was personal, and he was way too invested.

Hank knew he had crossed a line, but this was his partner and his friend. "Come on. Let's go get coffee or ice cream or whatever. We'll ride by just to be sure. Besides, can't have your love-sick ass moping around here all night." Hank stood and waited for Trey to do the same.

Trey nodded and flipped the file closed. He stood up, "Maybe you're right. How much more could this really escalate? I mean, what comes after shots fired? An explosion of some kind?"

The buddy cops exited the station.

CHAPTER 15

Amelia sat seemingly alone, still bound to the witness chair. Dan had not made a sound recently. She had not heard any further movement from the darkened courtroom. Could Dan have left her? She was still restrained but with a little more time…

Then Amelia faintly heard the tapping of Dan texting on a cell phone. His voice deferred her hope and jolted her back to reality. "Ms. Melchor, I just have to ask... are we having fun yet? I know I am!" Dan appeared from out of a dark corner in the courtroom, walked to the prosecutor's desk and stood there glaring at her.

"Gee, I don't know. Let me duct tape you to a chair and we then can see how much fun it is," she thought to herself. She wanted to tell him where to go and how to get there, but she also knew how unstable he was. She needed to gain his trust if she was going to get out of this alive.

She started, "When a parent comes to me, and their marriage is falling apart, I try to do what's best for the child."

Dan slammed his fist onto the table. "When a marriage is falling part, you throw a hand grenade in the middle of it! No divorce, no payday, right? And as far as what's best?? In what universe do you think you could possibly know what's best for anyone but yourself?"

Amelia answered, "There's a lot of research showing that children do best when they're with their mo..."

Dan cut her off and moved toward her. "Is that so, counselor? Children thrive when they're taken from those monstrous beings also known as fathers?" He was standing under one of the few lights in the room. The way the shadow fell across his face he seemed a monster, or at best, a madman .

Amelia backpedaled, "I didn't say that. I --"

"You what, Ms. Melchor? You feel misunderstood?"

"There's a bond between mothers and their children and they --" Amelia stammered.

"A bond? Well, that's beautiful. Something a simple sperm donor like me is incapable of comprehending. Keep talking, counselor. You're stating my case quite succinctly. You don't work with clients. Clients are people. You work with statistics... Past experiences... Something you read in an article somewhere. It's not a reason, counselor. It's a means to an end... a payday!"

Dan wasn't done with his rant, "And that is to justify your atrocities within that black soul of yours. Isn't it true that you care more about 'the kill', than you do about the client?"

He lowered his voice and moved closer to her. "Unburden yourself, counselor. The truth can set you free! But then again, truth is a fluid concept to you!"

She explained, "I saw a family. A woman who wanted to be with her child... When a client hires me, I have to advocate for her."

"What child, counselor? Do you even remember her name?" Dan was wild-eyed and had a tone of disgust.

Amelia started, "I..."

"You just *had* to advocate for this poor child... my daughter... whose name you can't even remember?" Dan's eyes filled with tears, and he spat in disgust. "And you call me the monster."

~~~~~~~

Trey and Hank arrived at Amelia's law office in Trey's unmarked car. They walked up the sidewalk, surveyed the building and looked for anything out of place.

Hank noted, "The place is still in one piece; that's new.

Trey nodded in agreement, but continued to inspect the office windows and peered inside the door. Everything seemed to be alright, but his gut told him otherwise.

Hank was antsy. "Come on, partner. Let it go." Trey relented, against his better judgement, and headed back to his car.

A call from dispatch ended any interest Trey had in the building. The dispatcher announced, "Attention, unit seven. See the man at the Rosewick Hotel. Possible hit and run."

Trey picked up his radio and responded, "Copy that, dispatch. Unit seven en route, forthwith." He threw his car in drive and sped off, worried what he would find when he got there. "Amelia...."

CHAPTER 16

Dan wiped the drizzle of spit off of the corner of his mouth with the back of his hand, walked back to the table and picked up Amelia's business card. "Attorney at Law..." He ripped the card in two.

Amelia got frightened. She had no luck fighting fire with fire, so she tried another tactic, "You know, custody agreements aren't necessarily permanent. If there's been some miscarriage of justice, I'm an officer of the court. It's my duty to set it right."

Dan's amused chuckle turned into a full-on belly laugh which rang maniacal in Amelia's ears. She didn't get it.

"I was born at night, counselor, but it wasn't last night! You go back to that courthouse and tell them a case you tried was tainted in some way, and you know damn good and well that will call into question every single case, every judgment you've handled!"

He continued, "I never thought you had it in you, but now is a deadly time for sense of humor, counselor!"

She answered, "Then have your attorney request a hearing to change custody. I'll convince your wife it's in her best interest not to fight it! Happens all the time!"

"You have overplayed your hand once again, counselor. Not that your extreme overconfidence doesn't amuse me. But there's no way in hell you're going to get your client to change her mind."

Amelia thought she may have found a chink in his armor. Perhaps her guile was faring better than her bravado. "I don't know. It's my job to be persuasive. What makes you so sure I can't convince her not to fight your custody request?"

Dan's laugh turned to sarcasm, "Because, counselor, your client is dead!"

This revelation startled and then frightened Amelia. She reacted before she thought it through. Her self-righteous response belied her fear. "You didn't have to kill her! There was another way!!! You really are a monster." Amelia intuitively realized that if he had murdered his wife, he would have no compunction about adding her death to his resume.

Dan moved closer to her and pointed his finger in her face, "Oh a monster definitely killed my wife. But that monster was you, counselor!"

His words hit her like a sledgehammer, "You're insane! I'm in no way responsible for your wife's death." She was now confused and visibly shaken.

"As surely as if you pulled the trigger yourself."

She suddenly realized she was in more danger than she had imagined. He thought she was the reason his wife was now dead. Motive for murder number two.

She came to herself; a change in strategy. She tried reasoning with him. "How can I possibly have killed her when I didn't even know she was dead until 20 seconds ago? Think it through!"

"You didn't know she was dead because she was just a paycheck to you. You'd have to actually care about someone to follow up with them once the check has cleared the bank." There was a coldness in his voice that further unnerved her.

"I work with a lot of clients... " she tried to explain.

"You deposit the check and move on to the next one. You'd have to actually be a human being to consider the look of fear in my daughter's eyes."

"Fear?" she asked.

"When you took her from me at the courthouse and *made* her leave with her mother. She was afraid." Dan's voice was now booming in her ears. "My daughter, my child. What's her name?"

"Her name?" Amelia was stalling. She had no idea.

"You decided her fate without a thought of the consequences! What's... her.... name?"

Amelia couldn't pretend; she didn't know.

"Her name is Eve." Dan said, coldly.

"Eve," Amelia said her name softly.

Dan pointed the pistol at her again. "Eve was afraid. Say it."

"Eve was afraid." Amelia complied.

"I made Eve afraid, say it!"

Amelia responded, "I made Eve afraid."

"I put Eve in danger, say it." Dan demanded.

"I don't understand..." Amelia stated, still confused.

Dan wagged the gun at her. "Say it. I put Eve in danger."

"I put Eve in danger."

"I destroyed the man in front of me."

Amelia pleaded, "Sir, I don't have the power to... "

"SAY IT. I destroyed the man in front of me."

"I destroyed the man in front of me," she obeyed.

"His name is Dan," he ordered.

"His name is Dan."

"His wife was Marah."

She repeated, "His wife was Marah."

"Their daughter is Eve." He was getting weak.

"Their daughter is Eve."

Dan turned away from her and began to weep softly. Could this be a breakthrough? He was silent for a few minutes. Was it over? The glimmer of hope faded.

He composed himself before turning back to her. She needed to understand some things. "You and I. We've met before," he said. "Before today. Before court."

"I…" she drew a blank.

"Where did you meet me before the trial?" Dan pressed. He stared into her eyes, as he waited for her reply.

Amelia dug deep into the darkened corners of her mind. There it was! She remembered the day she was in court with Marah. She recalled Dan walking in with his attorney and standing at the defendant's table. She *did* remember him from before that moment. Her attention came back to the room and the man in front of her. She glanced at him in a moment of recognition. Amelia then cast her gaze downward, wracked with guilt.

"Ah, what's this?" Dan asked.

"You came to my office. Ex parte."

Dan lowered the gun. "Why was I there?"

She attempted to explain. "You... wanted to talk to me... regarding the divorce... but I couldn't... "

"No ex parte communication allowed," he recalled, matter of factly. "That's what you said."

"It's against the judicial Code of Ethics." She replied.

"Ethics. That's another fluid term, isn't it? Ms. Melchor, do you remember what I told you?"

"I'm sorry. I don't..."

Dan was losing his patience. "Think hard!"

Amelia's mind was all over the place.

~~~~~~~~

Amelia looked up from her desk to see Dan standing in the doorway of her office. He was much softer than the man holding a gun over her in the present. Sad. Broken. He lightly tapped at the door. He addressed her, "Ms. Melchor..."

She was cold. "May I help you?"

Dan extended his hand, "I'm Dan. Marah's husband."

"Sir, you can't be here. I have to ask you to leave, or I will be required to report this incursion to the court." She waived him off, completely dismissing him, and returned to her work.

Dan stepped further into her office and stood in front of her desk. "Ms. Melchor, I need to talk to you about Marah. It involves the safety of our daughter."

Amelia glanced up at him, disinterested in hearing his plea. "Have your Attorney send me a letter."

He was determined. "It's about her drinking."

Amelia stood up; she was not about to get involved in his scheme. "Sir, I'm going to have to insist that you to leave my office immediately."

"Our daughter is frightened when she's with Marah," he pleaded.

Amelia picked up her phone receiver and pressed a button. "Yes, can you come help remove someone from my office?"

"Ms. Melchor, I'm begging you to listen to me."

"Your wife is my client. Not you. Her parents insist that this be handled discreetly; however, you are about to make that quite impossible."

Dan was adamant. "Your client needs help! Look, I'm not trying to take Eve away from her. I'm just asking you to help her seek treatment."

His appeal fell on deaf ears and was cut short by the two security officers who took him by the arms and led him out.

"Thank you," she nodded to the men. Her final comments to Dan were, "We'll see you in court."

Dan struggled to shake the men off of him, "Please don't do this!"

~~~~~~~

Amelia shifted her attention back to the courtroom and her predicament. "I'm sorry, I don't remember."

"Don't? Or won't? Apparently, money buys tainted verdicts *and* selective memory loss. You knew she had a drinking problem! I came to you, pleaded with you! But you were paid off by my mommy and daddy dearest to sweep it under the rug, make it go away!"

He continued without stopping, "You threw me out of your office, then threw me under the bus in open court. No consequences, no guilt, you went back to your office and put the check in the bank. But no matter how many times you wash your hands, you'll never get them clean. Welcome to your consequences!"

"We can't just take your word for something. That's for a court to determine. Estranged husbands say all kinds of things," Amelia explained.

"Estranged? You knew what I wanted? I wanted my wife back: sober! I didn't want the damn divorce. You pushed her into this! Right into harm's way!"

Amelia pleaded, "Sir, I'm sorry. I don't…"

Dan cut her off, "I wanted Marah to get help. I wanted us to be a family again." He glared at her, evil. "But you! You ruined everything; you single-handedly destroyed us!"

Amelia listened to his words, but they were *not* what frightened her. She knew there would be consequences, and she could only imagine what would happen next. Whatever that was, she became keenly aware of her growing impotence to stop it.

CHAPTER 17

Trey's cruiser barreled down the community streets, lights flashing. He turned into the Rosewick Hotel parking lot and spied Amelia's wrecked BMW with the driver's side door open. Trey's unit screeched to a halt, and the partners launched from the vehicle.

"Dammit, girl. You always know better! Now what?" Trey took in the scene with lightning speed. His years on the force had sharpened his ability to recognize clues.

"I'll call CSU and check security footage," Hank pulled out his phone and started punching numbers.

Trey scanned the parking lot. "You see something I don't? There's not a camera in site!"

Hank replied, "Maybe they're trying not to announce it. What about the ATM camera across the street?" He tried to be positive for his partner. I'll check it out; you do a quick canvas. We need focus; the clock is ticking!"

Trey's brow was furrowed and a deep scowl donned his face.

Hank reassured him, "And Trey… keep the faith. We'll find her." He turned and hurried toward the hotel entrance.

~~~~~~~

Amelia tried her best to compose herself. She believed her wits were the only thing that could stall the inevitable and give her a chance for intervention and rescue. She wanted to win his trust. Keep him talking, not shooting. "Look. I know this is hard. I'm sorry for the loss of Marah. Tell me where your daughter is now. Let's think about how to fix this."

Dan's laugh was sinister. "You're a real piece of work, Amelia Melchor, Esquire." He let out an angry sigh. "Eve suffered under the care of her mother. Marah was a functional alcoholic for the most part, but graduated to a 'black out' drunk after the divorce."

His anger escalated, "Do you know what that does to a five year old little girl? Left to fend for herself, in a constant state of fear!?!"

Dan's glaring stare made it difficult for Amelia to remain calm. She kept her voice low and soft, "I can imagine that was very hard for her. But that's a family matter. I'm just an Attorney. There's a process..."

"You can imagine? When she was with my wife, my daughter never felt safe in her own home! She lived in constant fear in the one place in the whole world she needed to feel secure!"

Amelia responded, "Look. I'm not perfect. But I can help you get your child back."

"Oh, we'll be together... before this is over." Amelia was taken aback by his statement. Had he really thought that far ahead?

Amelia tried to reason with him further. "What's your plan? You have zero chance of success with me *here*, like this."

Dan's icy stare cut into Amelia. "Pain unfathomable. Depression unthinkable. Loss unbelievable. All caused at your hand. You are exactly where you deserve to be."

The tension was getting to her, and she was ready for this to be over. Suddenly their cell phones chimed. Amelia screamed.

Dan picked up Amelia's phone and grinned as he looked it over. "Well, well, well."

Amelia squirmed and twisted her restraints. "What is it?"

"It seems someone noticed your absence." Only Dan realized this was no accident.

Amelia leaned toward him and strained to see the screen.

Dan kept the phone out of her gaze. He read the notice to her instead, as a reminder that he was in control: "Police searching for newly announced candidate for Judge, fear foul play involved." Dan paused for effect. "We are just now getting to the foul part..." He trailed off, as he typed a message on her phone as though there were some internal musings.

~~~~~~~

Elsewhere, Trey knocked on the front door of Amelia's house, while Hank went around back. Her car wasn't there obviously; the lights were out, and there didn't appear to be anyone inside. He banged louder and shouted to her, "Amelia! Amelia!"

His cell phone chimed with an incoming text message. It was Amelia's message tone, and he quickly opened it. It was a picture of her, bound to a chair. The note attached read, "Think of it as a mercy killing."

Trey raced back to his car calling for Hank. "Partner, we gotta go… now! Hank ran to the unit, and the two of them headed back to the precinct.

CHAPTER 18

In the dank and desperate courtroom, Dan pocketed the cell phone and put the gun between Amelia's eyes again. "I just texted your boyfriend, the cop."

Amelia played it cool. "Ex. That's been done for a while. He's a bit too clingy, so I kicked his thin blue line to the curb."

Dan didn't buy it. "You couldn't tell the truth if it bit you in the ass! I've done my homework, Ms. Melchor. I wasn't prepared for you the first time we met. I wasn't going to make that mistake again."

He jostled the pistol around in his hand as he spoke, "I know everything you care about, and I know everyone who cares about you. And you are all going to suffer, just like I've suffered, like Eve suffered!"

His agitation peaked, as he pressed the gun to her head once more. Amelia shut her eyes tight and braced herself. Tears rolled down her cheeks.

"Suffer!" yelled Dan. CLICK! Dan pulled the trigger again, empty chamber number two.

Amelia let out a whimper; then her fear turned to anger. "All this pussyfooting around is getting old and vastly unoriginal."

"Sorry if I'm boring you, counselor." Dan flashed the gun in her face. "But I think sooner, rather than later, you're going to have a very open mind about all of this". Dan laughed maniacally at his turn of phrase.

~~~~~~~

The police department phone lines were buzzing with tips. Officers were mulling over the social media responses to the news alert about the missing attorney.

Trey stood up from his desk and confronted Hank. "How can you expect me to sit here after getting a text like this? It's from *her* phone! She's been taken!"

Hank responded, "You know the drill! Would you let a civilian go off half-cocked? What would you tell him? 'Ride around the city with your head out of the window screaming her name?'"

"Better than sitting on my thumbs," he retorted.

"What a bonehead play!" Hank's comment snapped Trey back to reality. "I told you, you're head's all over the place where she's concerned. Keep it together, partner! Start thinking like a cop, or someone's gonna end up dead."

Trey came to himself; Hank continued. "The tech geeks are on it! I need you to have a clear head when they give us a location. Now cool your jets for just a while longer."

CHAPTER 19

Amelia sat frozen in fear; Dan had become more agitated and unhinged. She noticed his breathing was more erratic, and he was pacing around the room. She sat silently watching him as he narrated his plan for her. The lack of control was breaking her.

"I can't speak for you, but I've enjoyed our little remedial lesson in fear. Time to take it to the next level." Dan savored the moment. "Fear. There's a lot of power in it. Some people are afraid of spiders. Some people are afraid of guns. Some people are afraid to die. Personally, I have come to embrace it."

Dan paused for a few breaths for dramatic effect. He had planned this entire scenario, and for the most part it had gone according to that plan. He was in the moment. He continued his rant, "What about you, counselor? Do you ever wonder about the day you'll die?"

Amelia followed him with her eyes but didn't answer. She considered her options, and silence was the best course for the time being.

"There are few days in our lives that own that kind of significance, the day you become worm food." Dan looked the gun over as though it was a tool in the hands of a craftsman. "Do you think we know when our time is up? When all of your vain pursuits become the lining of your coffin?"

"That dash between the date you were born and the day you die. Then your legacy is set in stone, counselor, like the marker on your grave."

Dan stepped closer to Amelia to impress upon her the magnitude of his words. He glared at her with grave intent. "Just what do you think your legacy is going to be, Ms. Melchor?"

She remained silent and he continued. "Because I can guarantee you, without fear of contradiction, that Amelia Melchor, Attorney at Law, is about to come to her end."

Amelia's need to control got the better of her. She called his bluff, "No one is dying here tonight! I see it now. You're getting your rocks off by putting me through your personal campaign of terror! What happens in this room, right here, right now is your word against mine. And I don't think..."

"You think *too much of yourself* is what you think." Dan interrupted her with great prejudice. He stepped closer, asserting his authority. "I promise you, you are done tonight; and I keep my promises." His reign of fear wasn't over.

"If I die tonight, your case won't get reopened. No. Because if I die right now, you don't get closure. You're a smart man. Angry. Perhaps rightly so. But you're smart. And you know that if I die you go behind bars. Then what happens to your daughter? What happens to Eve?"

Dan lost his cool and lunged at Amelia, who gasped uncontrollably. "I'm about sick of hearing my daughter's name escape your lips." The volume of his voice increased as he continued. "You have lost the privilege of speaking her name."

Murder wrote itself across Dan's face. That was not the plan, at least not right now. He checked himself. "Concerning yourself about my daughter, at this moment, is terrible timing on your part!"

"Why is that? I think you're the one who is afraid. I think you're scared out of your mind that you can't be the father that you make yourself out to be." Amelia was grasping at straws and could risk taking a hit to find a point of emotional leverage.

"I think you're all talk and no show!" she reckoned, calling a bluff on this deadly game of cards. "I think the one who needs to be worried about legacy here is you! What kind of legacy are you going to give your daughter from the jail cell they toss you in when this is over?"

Amelia was feeling brave, not willing to fold just yet. "And I don't have to be afraid of you, you little man. Because Trey is going to come for me. And when he does, he's going to bury you. Your only play is to let me go, and you might survive this."

Dan's scowl turned into a grin. "Your boyfriend *is* gonna come rescue you? I'm counting on it! I told you I'm going to hurt you and everyone who cares about you."

Dan calls her hand and goes all in. "Like I said, I've done my homework."

Amelia suddenly felt fear to the depth of her core. She shook involuntarily. It was one thing to hurt her, but now he talked about hurting everyone close to her. Trey could take care of himself, but what about Angela and the boys? Were they on that list too?

"Are you afraid now, counselor? Sitting there helpless to save yourself and someone you care about." Too many scenarios ran through Amelia's mind. None of them ended well. She was forced to deal with the ramifications of her past deeds. What could she do at this moment to affect the past?

Tears spilled out of her eyes and down her cheeks. She wanted to hurt him now but was helpless. "I..." she started, but couldn't find words to express herself without revealing her terror.

"Feel it, Amelia. Fear." He moved so close to her, she could feel his breath on her face. She closed her eyes and tried to shut him out.

"Do you feel fear, Amelia?"

She nodded and whispered, "Yes."

"Good. That fear haunts me every day. But Eve knows it at a depth I can't bear to fathom."

~~~~~~~

Five year old Eve walked into the living room of her house. The front door was wide open, and the only light in the room was the TV, which was blaring loudly. Eve closed the front door and locked it. She then knelt by her mother, who was passed out on the couch. It was dark out, and Eve was afraid.

She shook her mother. "Mommy, wake up. Mommy, please." Marah didn't stir, and Eve began to cry. "Mommy, I'm hungry. Mommy..." Eve laid her head on Marah's chest and listened for a heartbeat, a sign of life.

"It's okay Mommy, I'll get help." Eve picked up the house phone and dialed a 9.

Suddenly, Marah stirred and changed position on the couch. She slurred her words, "S'okay baby. Fix pbj..." She passed out again.

Eve laid the phone back on the coffee table. Fear turned to sadness. She knew the drill. Mommy's little soldier trudged toward the kitchen. Once again, the child had to fend for herself.

~~~~~~~

In the wee hours of the morning, Marah was passed out on the couch again, still in her street clothes from the day before. Eve struggled to carry the bowl of cereal, overflowing with milk, into the living room. Eve approached Marah, spilling cereal and milk onto the floor, and tugged on her mother's hand. Marah didn't move.

"Mommy," Eve called out to her. "Mommy, we have to leave soon. I don't want to be late for school again. Teacher said I can't."

Eve sat the bowl of cereal down on the coffee table. She picked up one of Marah's shoes off the floor and tried to put it on her mother's foot. When that didn't work, she took Marah's hand and tried to pull her off the couch. Marah waived her away, like she was a pesky mosquito.

Eve continued to tug at her mother's arm.

~~~~~~~

"Eve was never safe with Marah," Dan spoke the words like he was outside of himself. He told her the stories of how poorly Eve was treated by Marah, as Eve had told him during his brief visits with her. Dan became numb.

Amelia looked down at the floor. "I didn't know. I'm so sorry to hear that."

Dan was enraged again, "Sorry? That was every day of her life. Marah was unfit! I came to you, hat in hand. I tried to tell you that. And you refused to talk to me. Too late for 'sorry'!"

Amelia started to crack. The onslaught of blame and his relentless terror had begun to take a toll on her. "I didn't know," she repeated, defeated.

"You didn't want to know! You were too busy finding ways to discredit me and cover up my wife's alcohol abuse to even consider my daughter's situation. That didn't pay the bills."

He kept piling it on. "She was five. She was a pawn in your shell game. Giving Marah full custody, you robbed Eve of her innocence. You killed her childhood."

All she could say was, "I didn't know."

Dan saw her breaking but continued undaunted. "Do you know what it's like to live in fear in your own home? To be afraid of the person who's supposed to be taking care of you?"

Amelia nodded, solemnly. "Yeah, I do. Or did you think you had cornered the market on suffering?" She mustered up what little fight she had in her, "The man I loved, the man I trusted with my whole heart lied to me, stole from me, cheated on me and finally beat me. So yes, I know a little something on that subject."

"Objection! Facts not in evidence. The fact is, Eve was five. You were a grown woman with choices, and you stayed." He leaned in to her. "And what does that say about you?"

"It says I couldn't get far enough away from my husband for the bastard not to find me. And after the third time he dragged me back home, I lost my will to fight it. I lost my dignity, and I lost myself."

~~~~~~~

The lights were off in the large house. What started as a low rubble grew louder and more articulate. A woman screamed!

The aggressive jingle of keys led to the door opening. The light from the front porch silhouetted Davis and Amelia. He had her by the hair, and he flung her inside, to the floor. Amelia landed with a thud.

Davis turned on the inside lights with his left hand and pulled a massive Colt Python from behind his back with his right. Davis acted and moved like an impaired maniac, not completely in control of his faculties.

"You think you can just leave me anytime you please?" Davis slurred. "You couldn't survive a day without me, you stupid cow!" Amelia was neither of those things, but Davis said them often enough that there was doubt in her heart.

He waved the huge revolver around with a bit too much abandon. Amelia pleaded; Davis enjoyed it, "Davis please…" Amelia had been beaten; however the worst of it was not physical, but emotional.

"You took a vow before God and our families to stay 'til death' do us part!" Davis stammered. He pulled the hammer back on the .45 and moved his finger to the trigger. "If you're ready to part, I'm happy to help."

Amelia groveled; Davis doubled down. "If you ever just leave like that and embarrass me again, I will shoot you in the face! You're a disgrace!" Davis waved his pistol to indicate the entire home.

"This house is a disgrace! You're trying to shame me in front of my mother." Davis rambled incoherently in a random stream of unconsciousness.

Amelia attempted to break through his diatribe, "I love you, Davis. You need help. Let me get you some help."

Davis walked over to her, grabbed her by the hair and stood her up! "You can help me! Do your job and clean this filthy house! It's enough that I tolerate your fat ass! If you won't keep yourself up, the least you could do is keep this house up... and serve me a hot meal once in a while."

Davis sent her off with a swift kick in the pants. Amelia almost hit the floor again. "We're married, Amelia, which basically means I own you," Davis insisted. "This is your life, forever! Get used to it!"

~~~~~~~

Dan was unmoved by her story. His anger cut right through her. "So then I became your outlet. And my daughter became your casualty. It was about payback, plain and simple." Dan was disgusted, "Well, pin a rose on you."

Amelia nodded, a little more understanding. Then deflected and looked away.

CHAPTER 20

Marah's place continued to erode. The house was filthy, as was Eve, though she tried as well as any five year old could to keep up appearances.

"Mommy wake up, I have to go to school." Eve tugged at her mom.

Marah rolled over slightly and opened her eyes. "What Eve? What do you want now?"

"We have to go to school today. It's Tuesday," Eve replied.

Eve pulled on Marah again. Marah rolled over and pushed Eve to the floor. "Stop pulling on me! Alright, Eve. I'll take you to the damn school."

Eve sniffed as she tried to hold back tears.

Marah opened her eyes and saw the spilled cereal on the floor. "What the hell? You spilled cereal? Damnit, Eve. Get that out of the living room."

Eve quickly gathered up the cereal bowl and took it to the kitchen. "I'm sorry, Mommy. Please don't be mad."

Marah sat up and propped her elbows on her knees, face into palms, and rubbed her aching head. She reached over and picked up her cell phone off the coffee table and looked at the time. "Shit."

Marah begrudgingly made her way off the couch and stumbled into the kitchen where Eve had dropped the whole bowl of cereal and was trying to clean it up. Marah let out a deep sigh. "God, Eve."

Marah looked at the mess on the stove. "I've told you not to try to cook."

"I was hungry, Mommy," she apologized.

Marah was annoyed. "PB&J! No cooking!" Marah opened the cabinet and pulled out a Pop Tart box. She shook it upside down. Empty. Marah came to herself briefly, "I'm sorry, baby. Mommy's gonna do better."

Marah pulled Eve to her. Eve hugged her tight. "I love you, Mommy."

"I love you too, baby." The moment didn't last. "Time to go. Come on, let's get you to school." Marah was still wobbly as she took Eve's hand. Marah was not completely sober at the moment.

~~~~~~~~

Amelia became overwhelmed. Dan turned toward her and laid blame, "You brought my daughter nothing but misery in Marah's custody! That's a fact that you're gonna have to swallow!"

Amelia was angry and spoke through tears, "You keep laying this at my feet! I'm an attorney, not a goddam social worker! Where the hell was your attorney? Where were *you*?"

Dan looked at the empty Judge's seat. "Permission to treat the witness as hostile, your Honor?" He turned back to Amelia. "My attorney was fresh out of law school. He couldn't find his ass in the dark with both hands and you drowned him in depositions and motions. You made sure he was all I could afford because you had our joint account frozen."

A single tear rolled down Amelia's cheek.

"As for me? I was a basket case. My world was falling down around my ears. I naïvely believed that I could count on you, an officer of the court, to do the right thing for Marah. That's why I came to your office."

Amelia began to sob. That seemed to anger Dan even more. He began a self-loathing rant.

"I admit it, counselor. I was weak and it cost me everything! So I waited and I watched. I studied everything about your life. I've read and copied every confidential file you have. I know where the bodies are buried now, counselor! I know your weaknesses and I exploited every one of them to get you right here, right now!"

Dan put the pistol to Amelia's head once again. "You murdered my life one piece at a time. I'm taking yours the same way."

Amelia closed her eyes tight as Dan pulled the trigger. CLICK! This time she didn't even flinch.

"Apparently we're not done for today." Dan spoke with no emotion in his voice. Cold. He turned and walked away from her. Amelia sobbed uncontrollably. She could barely hear Dan texting in the darkness a few steps away from her.

~~~~~~~

Trey stomped impatiently around his precinct's technical unit. "C'mon, Joe. Anything new on that text?"

"It was her cell, alright," Joe replied, not looking up from his computer, and continuing to type.

"So where is she?" Trey queried out loud, frustrated.

"We don't know yet," Joe stated.

"What do you mean you *don't know yet*?"

"GPS was off or disabled." Joe looked up at him and shrugged.

Trey sighed and threw up his hands. "You geniuses better figure something out! We're standing here with our thumbs up our asses while an innocent woman is out there severely wounded or dying."

Joe began typing faster on his computer.

CHAPTER 21

Amelia hung her head, still shaken. Dan was not moved by her tears. This is what he wanted. Success was within his grasp, and he was not letting up. "Oh, how the mighty have fallen. I guess pride really does come before a fall. Wouldn't you say, counselor?"

"And who is the prideful one here? The one duct taped to the witness stand? Or the one standing over her with a hand gun and a God-complex? Your daughter must be the envy of her classmates!" Amelia snarled.

She infuriated him again. Any attempt at sympathy was now gone. "Really? What do you think you know about Eve? Do you think you can even begin to understand her, the depth of what she went through after hearing a few sad moments of her existence? Don't even try!"

Dan began jostling the gun around again. Amelia's eyes widened with fear. "You're beginning to care on the wrong side of this thing, counselor! Damage done!"

"No! Damage is what happens to a little girl when she finds out her daddy has done something particularly heinous. Damage is what happens when your little girl sees her daddy's face on the front page of the newspaper or the lead story of the evening news. I've made my mistake and I'm paying for it dearly. Should you go through with all of this, you bring this to its final conclusion, then that damage is on you."

Dan laughed loudly, if not somewhat forced..

Amelia was incredulous. What was wrong with this guy? "You're insane! I'm giving you a way out of this and all you can do is laugh? We can fix this! Don't you want to save your daughter?"

Dan snapped and deliberately rushed at Amelia like a freight train, pushing the pistol down on top of her head once more. "My daughter's dead! My little girl, who suffered at her mother's hand, is gone because you put her there! And none of your double talk or legal posturing is going to save her now."

Realizing Dan now had no tether to this world, Amelia truly feared for her life and especially her loved ones for the first time. At the most, there are only three pulls left on that trigger. When she's gone, what would keep him from going after Angela?

~~~~~~~

Marah, still drunk from the night before, aggressively drove the car, with Eve bracing herself in the back seat. Marah began veering off the road, heading towards the ditch. Eve screamed, "Mommy! The road!"

Marah swerved hard back onto the road. As she did, she overcompensated and almost hit another car. The other driver laid on the horn. Marah yelled at Eve, "Don't yell at Mommy like that, you hear me?"

Eve nodded and tensed up, still bracing herself. Marah continued driving roughly without slowing down. Eve tried to get her mom's attention, she was afraid for her life.

She told Marah, "I love you, Mommy."

"I love you too, baby. What's a matter?" She looked in the rear view mirror at Eve.

Eve answered, "Your driving scares me."

Marah slammed her hand against the steering wheel. "Eve, if you don't shut up about everything you dislike about me, I'm going to pull this car over and give you one more reason to whine. Do you hear me? Hush! We're late enough. Mommy doesn't need any more distractions."

Eve looked up to see the traffic light they were speeding towards turn red without Marah slowing down. Eve screamed again, "Mommy!"

CRASH! Marah's vehicle made it halfway through the red light only to be t-boned by a garbage truck. The massive vehicle slammed into Eve's side of the car before the driver could even tap the brakes.

Marah's car spun uncontrollably then rolled over on its side. When the smoke finally cleared, everything was mangled and in a blur. Just parts of metal and glass everywhere. Marah laid on her back against the ground. Shards of glass fell to the asphalt as she turned her head to look for Eve. She screamed for her "Eve! Eve! Oh shit. Eve!" There was blood on the seat where Eve once sat.

~~~~~~~

After she learned of Eve's demise at the hand of her mother, Amelia slumped in the witness chair. The pistol pressed against her head seemed to crush her.

"No more birthdays, no more Christmas's. No more hugs and butterfly kisses. Only emptiness. Only pain." Dan's hurt and anger were palpable. "You did that to her! By an act of your will, you put in motion the events that would take her from us! OWN IT!!!"

As his fury came to climax, Dan let out a primal scream. Amelia's eyes shut against it, and tears streamed down her face. CLICK! Amelia jerked in her seat; she had fully expected a bullet. She couldn't take much more.

"Relax, counselor. We're nearly done here. Only two rounds left. Your odds are good." He stepped away from her and focused on her phone again.

CHAPTER 22

Trey was hovering over Joe's shoulder when Hank walked in. "Anything new?" he asked.

Trey shook his head, "This lunatic just keeps popping up like a prairie-dog! It's like he's dropping crumbs for us to follow, then..." Trey pantomimed a "poof".

Hank noticed Trey's de-escalated intensity and softened his tone, "Look, the things I said earlier…"

His attempt was met with an icy look from Trey.

Hank didn't give up. "I know you, partner. This is obviously personal. Too personal. And you know she's never going to give you anything in return. Not anymore."

Trey answered, "Her ex-husband was the bad guy here. She lived with that for a while after. It wasn't her fault."

"And you put yourself in harm's way to save her. That makes you a hero. The Chief said so himself."

His words gave Trey a chill. "Killing a man is not heroic."

Hank consoled him, "Not that same tired ass song again. IA cleared you; it was a righteous shoot. I'm just saying that you've punished yourself enough over..."

"Really? And exactly what is the statute of limitations for the guilt of taking a life?" Trey wasn't swayed.

~~~~~~~

Red and blue police lights flashed across the outside of the mansion-esque home in the early morning hours. Davis used Amelia as a human shield with his Colt Python to her head. Amelia had been beaten, this time more severely.

Sargent Trey Johnson trained his weapon on the troubled couple and attempted to diffuse the situation. Hank, his partner, stood at the passenger side of the police unit, gun laid across the roof at the ready to back Trey's play.

"Mr. Jefferson… Davis… you don't want to do this. There's a better way, an easier way. Just put the gun down and we'll all walk away. We can work this out."

Davis was manic. He was hopped up on something and, to him, his path was clear. "This is between my wife and me. We don't need you here. We don't need your interference! We were fine before you showed up."

Trey calmly insisted, "Mr. Jefferson, your neighbors were concerned. They called us to come help out, and that's what we're gonna do." Trey kept his vocal patterns nice and steady. He was careful not to provoke Davis into intensifying the situation. "Let's talk through this. Nothing's been done that can't be undone."

Davis went off. "Stop lying to me! I'm a lawyer. I know I'm going in the system. You're just trying to get me to trust you so your partner can shoot me down!" Things got tense.

"This is my wife! I have a constitutional right to bear arms. This isn't over until I say it's over!" Davis went off the rails, blathering. "You want to take her from me! You want to shoot down another black man!"

The irony of Trey and his partner also being black men was not lost on him. At that exact moment, however, it seemed pointless to debate it.

Amelia was in shock. She barely clung to consciousness. Davis continued his senseless rant.

"You can't do it! I won't let you! She's my wife! You can't take her! You can't take me! You can't kill me! I'll kill you first!" Amelia passed out and hit the ground hard. Davis pointed his weapon at Trey, fired and missed. Trey returned fire, striking Davis in the thigh.

Davis staggered; Trey demanded, "Gun down! Get on the ground! Do it now!"

Davis was all in. He looked at Amelia, passed out at his feet. In his impaired stated he raised his weapon one last time. Before he could get the shot off, Trey put a bullet center mass. Game over.

Trey ran to Davis and secured the Colt. Hank was on the radio calling for an ambulance. A second, then a third patrol car entered the scene.

Trey handcuffed Davis, then hurried to Amelia. He checked for vitals, hovering over her like lion standing watch over his pride.

~~~~~~~

DING! The computer in front of Joe interrupted the conversation. Joe was excited, "Hey guys... hold up! Her phone just came online again." He made a flurry of keystrokes. "Almost got it." Joe was in full geek mode. "Got it! Lexington and 17th, the old courthouse!"

Trey and Hank raced to the door before Joe's sentence was done.

~~~~~~~

Dan continued typing on Amelia's phone. This time, he didn't try to hide his handiwork from her.

This was new. She was curious. "What are you doing?"

Dan kept his eye on the phone as he spoke, "I believe some people will call it 'setting the record straight'. I told you I was prepared." Dan was intentionally cryptic, and he grinned.

Amelia got nervous. His silence was uncomfortable for her. "A remorseful confession? Nice touch," she baited. She could only hope.

"You might say that..." he said as he kept an eye on her phone. He was up to something. The fact that it upset Amelia was a bonus.

~~~~~~~

Back at the police station, Joe got another ding on his computer, as Dan's latest diatribe was intercepted. The communique appeared on Joe's desktop.

Joe picked up his cell phone and dialed Trey's number. "Detective, I'm screen sharing your perp's texts from Amelia's phone. He's texting someone at the news station."

Trey asked, "What's he saying?"

Joe replied, "Nothing like what you'd think! You're not going to believe this." Joe's eyebrows rose as he read the message to himself.

~~~~~~~~

Dan finished typing and gathered himself. He held Amelia's phone in one hand and the revolver in the other.

Amelia broke the silence, "I know you think of me as some kind of monster, but I'm sorry about your daughter."

Her words appeared to have no effect on him. "You're sorry because it brought you to this place. There's a difference between regret and remorse, counselor. But *you* know that, right? Every first week law student knows 'words have meaning'. And now you're finding out that actions have consequences."

"What do you want me to say? What's gonna satisfy this morbid sense of... ***personal justice***... you have going on in your twisted brain?" She had nowhere else to go and she was tired of it all.

"Bring back my daughter! Bring back my wife! That'll satisfy me. Apart from that, I've got nothing for you. But you're right, this is very personal."

Dan pulled out a photo of Eve and shoved it in Amelia's face. "Look at her! The face of innocence. She was five years old! Her last days on earth were filled with hurt and fear! So yeah, to me it's personal."

Dan brought Eve's picture back down and stared at it longingly. Amelia was sincere when she told him, "She's beautiful. But her mother? Did Marah die in the accident, as well?"

Her softness threw him for a moment. A haunted looked crossed his gaze. "Marah walked away with hardly a scratch; unharmed, at least physically. Losing Eve the way we did, I was furious, vengeful."

"But I had to forgive Marah. She was all I had left, the only piece of Eve still on this earth. I hoped the accident was a wake-up call and she'd finally get help." His voice was the softest it had been all day. His eyes widened in what must have been horror at the memory. He could barely articulate it.

~~~~~~~

Dan was on Marah's front porch, trying to calm her. She was drunk and stumbling. Dan reached for her. "Marah. We need each other right now. You're the only family I have left."

Marah jerked away and pointed her finger at him. "You're pathetic! I killed my baby! How can you still wanna be with me! How can you be anywhere near me?"

Marah stumbled backward, into the house she had shared with their daughter, slammed the door and locked it. Dan stared at the closed door, distraught. He banged on the door and yelled to her, "Marah, please. Let me in!"

He banged again with more fervor. "Marah, you're scaring me. If you don't open this door right now I'm going to have to call 911! Marah, please."

Inside, Marah looked around. All she saw were Eve's things amongst the disarray her home had become. Marah turned red-faced with shame and anguish. It was more than she could bare.

Dan heard her yelling from inside. "Goodbye, Daniel."

A moment later. BAM! A gunshot rang out and, Dan heard Marah's body hit the floor. Dan began slamming his shoulder into the door and screaming, "No! Marah, don't leave me!" He continued his assault on the entrance until, exhausted, he fell to his knees at the door.

CHAPTER 23

Dan was sadly stoic. "That's when I knew that forgiving Marah was the right thing to do. She blamed herself; but wasn't burdened with believing that I blamed her as well."

Tears streamed down Amelia's face. She knew she couldn't convince Dan of the remorse she felt and how devastated she was.

Dan continued, escalating, "But I knew then with great clarity the blame for the death of my wife and child belonged squarely in one place. Are you starting to get it, counselor? You understand now that you have to die! You're a danger to society. You subvert justice. You place more value on your warped personal priorities than the rule of law!"

Dan put the barrel of the revolver to Amelia's head once again. Less violent, less hate. Pitied. At this point, it is a mercy killing and Amelia agreed. "You have corrupted justice and ruined lives. My family is gone and I blame you!"

Amelia squeezed her eyes tight again as Dan pulled the trigger. CLICK! Amelia opened her red, swollen eyes. "Only one to go." He left her there, sweating bullets, and walked back to the prosecutor's table.

~~~~~~~

Dan maneuvered to a position behind the desk. He checked his watch. Time to end it. "As there is only one chamber left, I suppose it would be cruel and unusual to drag this out any longer."

Amelia nervously watched Dan as he walked toward her.

Dan started, "We'll now begin with the closing arguments. In the interest of fair play, is there a character witness you'd like to call? Anyone who would vouch for your integrity?"

Amelia shook her head and barely spoke above a whisper, "No." This was not the same Amelia Melchor, Esq. sitting before Dan as the one just hours earlier. He knew it.

He stood in front of her. "Amelia Melchor, I have demonstrated that every reasonable attempt was made to make you aware of the fact that my wife, Marah, was an alcoholic and as such was a danger to herself and her five year old daughter. And, failing to act in the best interest of the minor child, the life and safety of my daughter Eve was placed in jeopardy."

He continued, "Pursuant to such reckless endangerment and careless disregard for life, you did in fact cause the death of my wife and daughter."

Amelia listened in silence as he imposed his judgement.

"You were derelict in your duty to uphold the truth when you accepted blood money from Marah's parents to bury her addiction and refused her the treatment that she so desperately needed. In addition, you fabricated evidence in an attempt to assassinate my character to further your personal agenda of misandry and illicit gain. Your turn."

Amelia had nowhere to hide, nowhere to run. She sat in her remorse and held back tears of regret.

Dan stood a few feet away from Amelia. He raised the gun up with his arm outstretched and pointed it at Amelia's head. Amelia began to sob.

She looked up at him, faced her accuser and said, "I'm guilty."

Dan was caught off guard. He expected more excuses, more push back. What was her game? Maybe he misunderstood. "What? Say it louder for all the court to hear."

"I'm guilty. I did it. I did everything you said and more! I destroyed your family. I knew Marah had a drinking problem, but her family paid me extra to cover it up. I am guilty! I'm sorry, I'm so sorry!" Amelia surrendered, "I throw myself on the mercy of this court. Do with me as you see fit."

He slowly and deliberately walked to her and pressed the pistol to her head one last time. She closed her eyes.

Dan prepared his final judgement. "You have thrown yourself on the mercy of this court. In our mercy we sentence you to die!" Dan pulled back the hammer on the revolver, which he had never done before. Why was he hesitating? Was he unsure, having second thoughts? Amelia was ready for this! Was this his final act of cruelty, to make her wait? Excruciating!

A ruckus outside the courtroom took Dan's attention from Amelia. Suddenly, Trey and Hank burst through the door in the back of the courtroom, guns drawn.

Trey announced a warning, "Freeze! Put the gun down and step away from the hostage."

Dan's hand remained on the gun at Amelia's head. "Enjoy your next life, Amelia." Her eyes were fixed on Trey, begging him to save her. Dan turned around and aimed the gun at Trey.

He yelled to them, "I'm gonna kill her!"

Amelia shouted, "No!"

At that moment, her world went into slow motion. Trey and Hank didn't waste a second, and both fired at Dan, hitting him in the torso. Blood showered Amelia, and she screamed as Dan fell on the floor in front of her.

The two officers approached Amelia and Dan with guns drawn, trained on the perp. Dan writhed in pain.

Hank moved toward Dan and kicked the revolver away from his open hand. Dan tried to speak but could only manage a whisper. Hank knelt down at his side, leaned over and put his ear near Dan's mouth.

Trey went directly to Amelia, who seemed oblivious to Trey and at the same time consumed with Dan's condition. Trey spoke into his radio and called for an ambulance. "Dispatch, officer needs a bus at the old courthouse forthwith. Better make it quick, the perp is not likely."

Hank stood and turned to Trey. "No need for a bus, he's gone."

Trey pulled out his pocket knife and cut away the duct tape that bound Amelia. To Trey's surprise, she fell to Dan's side as he lay there dying. "No, Dan. *I'm* the guilty one! What did you do? No… you can't go! Not yet!"

While Amelia processed the moment, Hank checked the revolver and was surprised. He turned to Trey, "The gun is empty."

Amelia was also shocked. "No, I saw him load it. He put one bullet in the cylinder and left the other ones back there on the prosecutor's table."

Hank walked over to the table and moved Amelia's things around until he found a pile of bullets. "I don't know what she thought she saw. I count six bullets here on the table, partner. He never put it in the chamber."

Trey had seen that before. "Suicide by cop. Didn't have the guts to eat a bullet."

Amelia was still at Dan's side; his blood covered her hands. She recalled another piece of the puzzle. "Earlier he said that he would be together with his family before this was over. They are all dead. He wanted to be with his family." She sobbed as she spoke.

Trey asked Hank, "What did he say to you before he died? What'd he whisper to you? A dying declaration?"

Hank replied, "Yeah, you could say that..." He nodded toward Amelia. "It was a message for her."

That got Amelia's attention, and she quieted her sobs. "What did he say?"

"He said… he forgives you," Hank repeated, confused at the notion. "What does that mean?"

Amelia felt like she had been stabbed in her soul. That news broke her in a very deep place. She looked down at her blood-soaked hands and threw herself on top of Dan, gripping him tightly, desperately.

After a moment, Trey tenderly pulled Amelia off of Dan, which was difficult. She was drawn to Dan like an invisible magnetic force that compelled her. The ice queen had melted.

She gave in to Trey's pull and folded into him, clinging on for dear life. She sobbed deeply, as Trey held her. After a moment, Trey pushed her away. She looked up at him, confused as to why he didn't want her affection; the affection they had both so recently and fervently desired.

Amelia awaited some sort of declaration of romance or relationship. She certainly did not expect what Trey did next.

"Amelia Melchor, You are under arrest for witness tampering, suborning perjury, judicial misconduct... " He took her hand, turned her around and placed handcuffs on her. She felt for a moment that she had had some kind of psychotic break, but this was as real as it could be. She sobbed, as Trey Mirandized her. "You have the right to remain silent..."

She intermittently interrupted with, "I'm sorry. I'm so sorry." She walked with him, as he finished advising her of her rights.

Moments later, more officers and the crime scene unit poured into the courtroom and began processing the scene.

CHAPTER 24

One year later…

Amelia held a bouquet of flowers, as she stood in the cemetery. She stooped down and placed the flowers on the grave stone of Dan Schroeder. Marah rested on the far end of the plot, and Eve lay between them. Dan was reunited with his family.

She talked to Dan as if he could hear her. "I can't believe it's been a year already. So much has happened, I don't know where to start. So I guess the beginning will have to do."

She was softer now, more gentle in her speech. "I was arrested. Me! Handcuffed and booked. But I have a feeling you know that. After I was arraigned, I cut a deal. That's part how I was able to get you here together."

"I would have come by sooner, but... it's complicated. Anyway, Nothing is the same. I'm no longer Amelia Melchor, Attorney at Law. They removed the attorney part, thanks to you. And I have this nifty new jewelry." She pointed down to her ankle monitor hidden just beneath her pant leg.

"I really mean it, 'thanks'. I like my new life. I like who it's made me. I like who you made me." Her phone began to ring and just for a moment she thought it was a sign. She blushed and then answered, "Hello." She listened for a moment and then responded, "Ok... I'm on my way. No, I'm serious, I'm on my way." She smiled as she hung up her phone.

"I'm so sorry, Dan. I've gotta go. But now that I know where you are I promise I'll visit... often. For at least the next three to five years." She smiled at the thought of it. She turned and walked back toward Trey, who waited patiently for her. She stole a quick hug before getting into his car.

~~~~~~

Different courtroom, different day. Amelia stood at the prosecutor's desk inside the Family Courtroom. Next to her stood a woman, who was holding the hand of a child.

Amelia addressed the judge; "Your honor, I'm here with my colleague from the Court Appointed Special Advocates Office, Renee Weston, to represent the interests of the minor child, Rebecca Marie Lucas in the matter of custody between her parents. I have several exhibits to offer the court

Across the courtroom, Becky's mother and father each stood with their representative attorneys. They both glared at Amelia as she spoke to the Judge. Amelia felt their stares of disdain aimed at the back of her head, but then again, she was used to it. In this case, she was willing to take one for the team!

Renee smiled and handed Amelia several sheets of construction paper. A child's crayon drawings were etched on each them. Amelia in turn handed them to the bailiff. The images were disturbing, condemning drawings depicting Rebecca's family unit. "Your Honor, we are presenting these as exhibits D through J."

The Judge reached for the drawings and perused them for relevance.

The first drawing was of a child's stick figure family with mom drinking what looked like a beer and the child saying, "Mommy no!" The second was a stick figure child watching two stick figure adults fighting with a caption, "Don't hurt me!"

The third picture was a house with jagged lines representing angry shouts coming from the windows. A stick figure child sitting in the grass outside crying.

After the judge reviewed the evidence, Amelia addressed the court... "Your Honor, after exhaustive research and interviews with both of Rebecca's parents, it is our considered opinion that it is in the best interest of the minor child... "

The End

Made in the USA
San Bernardino, CA
19 October 2018